Tales of
Here & Then

Tales of
Here & Then

James Kelman

thi **wurd**

thi-wurd.com

First published in Glasgow, Scotland in 2020 by thi wurd

This edition first published in this format 2020 by thi wurd

Book only ISBN 978-1-8381030-2-6

eBook ISBN 978-1-8381030-3-3

British Library Cataloguing-in-Publication Data
A catalogue record for this book is available from the British Library

Cover design by Andrew Cattanach

Designed and typeset by Palimpsest Book Production Limited,
Falkirk, Stirlingshire

Printed and bound by Clays Ltd, Elcograf S.p.A.

James Kelman thanks Canongate Books Ltd.
and Tangerine Press for permitting the inclusion
of several stories from the collections
That was a Shiver and A Lean Third.

Preface

From the age of fifteen I was paid to study the page and how to compose. Ye learn to judge space, when a line is 'centred' incorrectly; typographical inconsistencies, spatial inconsistencies. In 1963 I became a member of the Scottish Typographical Association; I was coming up for seventeen. A year later, in Pasadena, California I passed the state entry test to become a journeyman compositor. In those days a compositor composed the page and was responsible for every aspect of that, including the space between letters, between words, between lines of words.

Is it 'space' or 'spaces'?

I discovered there is none. Every so-called 'space' was a piece of lead, some metallic compound, or wood, even plastic.

An apprentice begins by taking apart what the journeyman has composed; the page that has been printed, and distributes each and every piece of type back into its proper place within the case.

The Post-Impressionist painters not only created individual visual perspectives, the means they used were individual. They applied paint in a different way, they mixed it in a different way. It depends on the effect required or desired. A guitar is not interchangeable with a clarinet, or keyboard.

Everything is related: cause and effect, things don't stand alone: everything is something, and the compositor or the artist is responsible for everything, not just the words but the spaces between. Artists can't just leave the canvas blank. A blank canvas isn't nothing. Most artists are aware of this at least intuitively. Some never think about these things, they take it for granted we all share the same reality. The English and Anglo-American traditions are a bit like that. It's very convenient for the authorities, political and cultural. Not so in other intellectual traditions; related questions have been around for a while. The worlds of a starving child and one never without food, drink and shelter are entirely different.

Action can be back to front and inside out. The prismatic effect, seeing someone inside out, front and sides at the same time – a bit like Cubism.

What goes on in maths and science resonates in art. What do we mean by abstract, what do we mean by concrete? Every point is significant.

The thing in itself, the 100 percentness of any work of art – Brownian motion, the nature of the structure, notions of completeness – babble babble babble.

But it ties in with what we do in art, in prose fiction: set down a story that refers only to itself, utterly self-referential

which, of course, cannot happen, given the existence of other human beings.

For many a year I have wanted to see my short work gathered together in one book. In longer collections short tales may be missed. The majority here appeared in earlier collections, now out of print. Only two collections of my stories so remain: A Lean Third and That Was a Shiver. I thank Tangerine Press and Canongate Publishing for permission to use a few from them.

At least eleven of these are unpublished. They are not new stories to me. My policy is to bring a work to a conclusion. My aim is to know the conclusion and it may take a while.

for
Mandlenkosi Langa

CONTENTS

It was always her

On the Sunday before she was there by the window, she was central to it. Ours is a good-sized curved window, style Glasgow, with its alcove. The snow had fallen heavily for most of the morning and early afternoon and way way over down the Sandbank Street hill young folk were sledging and enjoying that snow, real snow, real deep and great and they were not used to it and prone to taking chances, young people gambling, life and limb; these thoughts dont enter their brain.

Snowman weather. They dont see much of that in Glasgow. A couple of days per winter they can bring out the sledges. Not much more. I'm saying this is how it was.

And her favourite radio station playing. So this was the Sunday, and the last quarter of an hour of the show. We listened to it most weeks. She it was. I wouldnt have bothered. She had her likes, she always did. This was good music, roots music, and the organist playing, a blues musician: Peterson maybe, that nice jazz-funk, reminiscent of old Jimmy Smith and she was standing gazing out, arms folded, swaying sideways to the music, her big woollen bootees, and the jogging trousers and the chunky cardigans, all relaxed here in her own home, while outside was beyond, beyond. These elements.

She had forgotten she was not alone.

It didnt matter anyway. If I had been a painter I would have had the pencil out, getting that shape, the light at the window, her rocking back and forth and on the window ledge the tall vase of flowers, while the flowers, orange/red tulips, not a big bunch, only a few stalks it looked to me, but what do I know. That song from 50 years ago young in my teens, going through my brain and I was smiling. Eventually she turned to do something, walk somewhere, go and do something – and she saw me, saw me smiling. She smiled too, a question.

No, I said, just eh . . . and that tune in my head that the way she looked was way beyond compare, how could I dance with another, when I saw her standing there.

That was how it was on the Sunday.

a Reader

; by rail daily to school, thus my penchant for departing class prior to the schoolday's rightful conclusion that I might not disintegrate through the unutterable boredom of the subjects under consideration, my being forced to consider these subjects that I might the better advance beyond my fellows on the hierarchical ladder that was the greatbritishsocialsystem, the place of my parents and family not deemed of the lower orders but affixed therein through no fault of our own howsomever the school subjects under consideration purported to bring about the opportunity of escape, nor yet the fault of my parents whose apparent acceptance of this greatbritishsocialsystem ceded to myself a marked nauseousness largely indescribable but by authors whose ability to transcend that same indescribability by virtue of the act of storytelling exhibited not only the sad limits of an inferior art but an open-armed adherence to that system, inducing within myself a consolidation of purpose, effected by that same nauseousness, the predictable outcome of right reasoning, my unconscionable assumption of the dubiety of all adult authority, my consequent contempt being ill-concealed, barely disguised, leaving withdrawal from that society my only duty, the last straw being the charred remains of a book I had purchased, found in the fireplace, having been adjudged licentious by my mother and set in flames, though the book were purchased on my own account by means of a monetary gift from a grandmother, that was mine and mine alone to do as wish should take me, so that now, approaching a birthdate of more than passing interest its being the age by which a youth may decree that the departure of the education system is the one route by which the guarantee of sanity may be

Acid

In this factory in the north of England acid was essential. It was contained in large vats. Gangways were laid above them. Before these gangways were made completely safe a young man fell into a vat feet first. His screams of agony were heard all over the department. Except for one old fellow the large body of men was so horrified that for a time not one of them could move. In an instant this old fellow who was also the young man's father had clambered up and along the gangway carrying a big pole. Sorry Hughie, he said. And then ducked the young man below the surface. Obviously the old fellow had had to do this because only the head and shoulders – in fact, that which had been seen above the acid was all that remained of the young man.

A History

When from out of the evening the quiet reached such a pitch I had to unlock the door and wander abroad. At this time the waves ceased pounding the rocks and the wind entered its period of abeyance. Along the shore I travelled very casually indeed, examining this, that and the other, frequently stooping to raise a boulder. That absurd and unrealized dream from childhood, that beneath certain boulders . . .

I was going south to south east, towards the third promontory. It was where I could take my ease at times such as this. A fine huddle of rocks and stone. There were three little caverns and one larger one, a cave; this cave would presently be dry. It always afforded a good shelter. From it I could gaze out on the sea. I withdrew my articles from my coat pocket, a collection of shells. Even now I retained the habit, as though some among them would prove of value eventually. I leaned close to the entrance of the cave and chipped them out in a handful, not hearing any splash due to the roaring of the waves. Yet there too had been a striped crab shell of a sort I was unfamiliar with, about five inches in diameter. I kept an assortment of items at home to which this crab shell might have proved a fair addition. In all probability, however, the stripes had simply been a result of the sea's turmoil. Or perhaps it had been wedged in between two rocks for several centuries. I doubted my motives for having thrown it away. But I had no history to consider. None whatsoever. I had that small collection of things and too the cottage itself, its furnishings and fittings, certain obvious domestic objects. But be that as it may not one of these goods was a history of mine. My own history was not in that cottage. If it could be trapped anywhere it would not be there. I felt that the existence of a dead body would alter things. Previous to this I had come upon a dead body so I did have some knowledge. It had been a poor thing, a drowned man of middle age, a seaman or fisherman. I made the trip to the village to convey the information then returned to the cottage to await their arrival. I had carried the body into there and placed it on the floor to safeguard against its being carried back out on the tide. The face was bearded, no boots on the feet though a sock remained on the left foot. A man in the sea with his wits about him, ridding himself of the boots to assist the possibility of survival. He would have had a family and everyday responsibilities whether to them or to his shipmates; that amazing urge to survive which is itself doomed. He would have been dead in twenty minutes, maybe less. If I had been God I would have allowed him to survive for twenty hours.

But now here I was. And could it be described as good, this lack of damp, not being chilled to the bone; even a sensation of warmth. All in all I was wishing I had kept a hold of the shells and that striped one of a crab, and I would then have been very content indeed, simply to remain there in the cave, knowing I would only have to travel such and such a distance back to the cottage.

The one with the dog

What I fucking do is wander about the place, just
going here and there. I've got my pitches. A few
other cunts use them as well. They keep out my road
cause I lose my temper. I've got two mates I
sometimes meet up with to split for a drink and the
rest of it. Their pitches are out the road of mine. One
of them's quiet. That suits me. The other yin's a gab.
I'm no that bothered. What I do I just nod. If
anybody's skint it'll be him. He's fucking hopeless. The
quiet yin's no bad. I quite like the way he does it. He
goes up and stares into their eyes. That's a bit like me
except I'll say something. Give us a couple of bob.
The busfare home. That kind of thing. It doesnt
fucking matter. All they have to do is look at you and
they know the score. What I do I just stand waiting at
the space by the shops. Sometimes you get them
with change in their hands; they've no had time to
stick it back into their purses or pockets. Men's the
best. Going up to women's no so hot because they'll
look scared. The men are scared as well but it's no
sexual and there's no the same risks with the polis if
you get clocked doing it. Sometimes I feel like saying
to them give us your jacket ya bastard. It makes me
laugh. I've never said it yet. I dont like the cunts and I

get annoyed. Sometimes I think ya bastard ye I'm fucking skint and you're no. It's a mistake. It shouldnt fucking matter cause you cant stop it. There's this dog started following me. It used to go with that other yin, the quiet cunt. It tagged behind him across in the park one morning and me and the gab told him to fucking dump it cause it must belong to somebody but he didnt fucking bother, just shrugs. One thing I'm finding but it makes it a wee bit easier getting a turn. But I dont like it following me about. I dont like that kind of company. I used to have a mate like that as well, followed me about and that and I didnt like it. I used to tell him to fuck off. That's what I sometimes do with the dog. Then sometimes they see you doing it and you can see them fucking they dont like it, they dont like it and it makes them scared at the same time. I'd tell them to fuck off as well. That's what I feel like doing but what I do I just ignore them. That's what I do with the dog too, cause it's best. Anything else is daft, it's just getting angry and that's a mistake. I try no to get angry; it's just the trouble is I've got a temper. That's what the gab says as well, your trouble he says you've got a fucking temper, you're better off just taking it easy. But I do take it easy. If they weigh you in then good and if they dont then there's always the next yin along. And even if you dont get a turn the whole fucking day then there's always the other two and usually one of them's managed to get something. That's the good thing about it, having mates. What I dont understand I dont understand how you get a few of the cunts going about in wee teams, maybe four or five to a pitch, one trying for the dough while the rest hang about in the background. That's fucking hopeless cause it just puts them off giving you anything and sometimes you can even see them away crossing the street just to keep out the way, as if they're fucking scared they're going to get set about if they dont cough up. It's stupid as well cause there's always some cunt sees what you're up to and next thing the polis is there and you're in fucking bother. What I think I think these yins that hang about in the background it's cause they're depressed. They've had too many knockbacks and they cant fucking take it so what they do they start hanging about with some cunt that doesnt care and they just take whatever they can get. If it was me I'd just tell them to fuck off; away and fuck I'd tell them, that's what I'd say if it was me.

of the spirit

I sit here you know I just sit here wondering what to do and my belly goes and my nerves are really on edge and I dont know what the fuck I'm to do it's something to think about I try to think about it while my head is going and sometimes this brings it back but only for a spell then suddenly I'm aware again of the feeling like a knife in the pit of my guts it's a worry I get worried about it because I know I should be doing things there are things needing doing I know I know I know it well but cant just bring myself to do them it isnt even as though there is that something that I can bring myself to do for if that was true it would be there I would be there and not having to worry about it at this stage my muscles go altogether and there's aches down the sides of my body they are actual aches and also under my arms at the shoulder my armpits there are aches and I think what I know about early-warning signs the early-warning signal of the dickey heart it feels like that is what it is the warning about impending strokes and death because also my chest is like that the pains at each side and stretching from there down the sides of my body as if I'm hunched right over the workbench with a case of snapped digestion the kind that has dissolved from the centre but still is there round the edges and I try to take myself out of it I think about a hundred and one things all different things different sorts of things the sorts of things you can think about as an average adult human being with an ordinary job and family the countless things and doing this can ease the aches for a time it can make me feel calm a bit as though things are coming under control due to thinking it all through as if really I am in control and able to consider things objectively as if I'm going daft or something but this is what it's like as if just my head's packed it in and I'm stranded there with this head full of nothing and with all that sort of dithering it'd make you think about you've got it so that sometimes I wish my hands were clamps like the kind joiners use and I could fasten them onto the sides of my head and then apply the thumbscrews so everything starts squeezing and squeezing

I try not to think about it too much because that doesnt pay you dont have to tell me I know it far too well already then I wouldnt be bothering otherwise I wouldnt be bothering but just sitting here and not bothering but just with my head all screwed up and not a single idea or thought but just maybe the aches and the pains, that physicality.

Cute Chick!

There used to be this talkative old lady with a polite English accent who roamed the betting shops of Glasgow being avoided by everybody. Whenever she appeared the heavily backed favourite was just about to get beat by a big outsider. And she would always cry out in a surprised way about how she managed to choose it, before going to collect her dough at the pay-out window.

And when asked for her nom-de-plume she spoke loudly and clearly: Cute Chick!

It made the punters' blood run cold.

Leader from a Quality Newspaper

It might well be wondered why certain hints of infinity are likely to knock folk back on their uppers. The answer lies not in hypocrisy but in genuine self doubt. Given the general mystification which hangs shroud-like from our shoulders we should not cry out when down falls the sword of an acquaintance. It is, after all, the sort of occurrence we are to be secure upon.

Governor of the Situation

I hate this part of the city – the stench of poverty, violence, decay, death; the things you usually discern in suchlike places. I dont mind admitting I despise the poor with an intensity that surprises my superiors. But they concede to me on most matters. I am the acknowledged governor of the situation. I'm in my early thirties. Hardly an ounce of spare flesh hangs on me – I'm always on the go – nervous energy – because my appetite is truly gargantuan. For all that, I've heard it said on more than one occasion that my legs are like hollow pins.

Our Times

There was this upper-middle-class fellow who was a genuine goody. Charles was his name. He may have been called after the English monarch. I did not know him personally and might have thought highly of him if I had. We shall never know. He was a boring individual in adult company but children suffered him and allowed him to join their games. On the whole his life was boring insofar as anyone's life is boring. But I was serious when I said I regarded him highly.

This will have the mark of authenticity about it.

Charles had a full-time upper-middle-class type of job. At the same time he was a complete individual, a whole human being, figuratively. So too was Sian, his wife. Sian is an unusual name for a woman which was of additional interest to myself, as is the Gaelic tradition.

Charles and Sian shared an interest in the arts and were at ease in their own community. This appealed to me. She was of the middling middle-class; a girl who, prior to the first pregnancy, held a responsible position in a local law firm. She would pick up her career where she had left off. Once her youngest child reached nursery-school age, she hoped. Sian was counting the months.

Theirs were decent children, neither stuck-up nor namby-pamby. They did not feel ill at ease if adults were in the same room yet had their own little circle of friends. They made no attempt to dominate mixed-age companies. Charles was proud of that. He disliked children being pushed to the fore in adult society. He thought it demeaning.

Sian thought the same but in her it occasioned pangs of guilt. In a curious way she was proud of that guilt. Yet the guilt itself was a secret and she disliked secrets. One night she blurted it out to Charles. His only reply was a smile. Sian liked his smile. It was beautiful. Oddly it was their daughter who inherited the smile. Sian wished it were the boy. Their smile reminded her of her own father and she had never much cared for him, nor his memory.

Twice a year the family holidayed together. These were not unadventurous forays and were thoroughly enjoyed. So much so that Charles and Sian intended selling up and moving abroad to a similar destination if only they could wangle early retirement. Times had become tough but they did stand a chance. I am not sure if ever they did wangle it. We only heard about them from neighbours. Each time I saw these particular neighbours it was not only a reminder but a rejoinder. It is true to state, therefore, given I was aware of the existence of Charles but fortunate in a circle of friends I could describe as 'mine' rather than 'ours', that the drama had yet to begin.

Bangs & A Full Moon

A fine Full Moon from the third storey through the red reflection from the city lights: this was the view. I gazed at it, lying outstretched on the bed-settee. I was thinking arrogant thoughts of that, Full Moons, and all those awful fucking writers who present nice images in the presupposition of universal fellowship under the western Stars when all of a sudden: BANG, an object hurtling out through the window facing mine across the street.

The windows on this side had been in total blackness; the building was soon to be demolished and formally uninhabited.

BANG. An object hurtled through another window. No lights came on. Nothing could be seen. Nobody was heard. Down below the street was deserted; broken glass glinted. I returned to the bed-settee and when I had rolled the smoke, found I already had one smouldering in the ashtray. I got back up again and closed the curtains. I was writing in pen & ink so not to waken the kids and wife with the banging of this machine I am now using.

```
                        Dear
                      o dear o
                      dear. And
                    yet she must
                   have been near
                   about 30 years
                     of age. But
                      a certain
                        pair
                     of legs have
                    the following
                   shape: slim over
                  the knees with the
                 sloped move down to
                the ankles which arent
                thick. She was wearing a
               miniskirt, and orange hair
               with rollers stuck in; about
          5'6"     in her red heels. And
          this     voice of an amazing
          kind     of hoarseness when
          first    I heard her in the
          shop     at the corner while
          she      asked for a pound
          of       brown sugar and 20
          of       your kingsize tips
          and      a box of cadbury's
          as       well Archie if you
                dont mind. And pushing
                out through the door
                she let it swing back
                as if leaving it for
                me. Against the wall
                 of her close she
                 was leaning as I
                 walked by clutch-
                 ing my golden vir-
                 ginia. And at 23
                years of age I was
               going through a bad
              patch with the
                    wife but
                    I did go
                    on past.
                    A couple
                    of days
                    later I
                    saw her
                    in the
                    street
                    bawling
                 at   some
               old timer:
               Ya  manky
              auld swine
              ye!  You
             still owe
              two  quid
              from last
                   week.
```

Leather Jacket

See you're okay because you've got a good leather jacket.

What you want me to feel guilty about it? I chuckled.

What's funny. Eh? what's funny.

Nothing.

What ye laughing about?

I'm no laughing. I'm just no going to feel guilty about it.

Sure. It's a personal decision.

What's a personal decision?

Guilt.

Guilt. I dont feel guilt – guilty, I dont feel it.

Guilt's aye personal.

What ye talking about?

Personal decisions, they're personal. I'm talking if one person makes it as opposed to a committee. Although committees are made up of people anyway, I'm talking individuals and personalities, etcetera.

. . .

Oh jesus fuck man it's cold innit. I dont fancy wearing the skins of dead animal but, definitely not.

Hide.

Hide yeh, I wouldnay wear that man. What time is it now?

Fuck knows.

Fucking dead animals man.

I know the arguments.

I know you know the arguments.

Aye well . . . I've no even got a smoke, have you?

Naw, that evil bastard man he used them for his ayn fucking shit then hardly gave us a drag.

. . .

I know ye know the arguments man so dont fucking, know what I mean, laying that at my door, fuck that man – I bought it down Camden Lock. She bought it for me and it was secondhand. Alright?

. . .

Alright?

Yeah yeah, sorry, it's just how some people think like if ye know them like it's a way to get rid of the guilt.

You've got guilt on the fucking brain man.

Oh I'm guilty I'm guilty and then ye dont have to do fuck all. Know what I mean, an actual course of action instead of just talking. What do ye call it, absolving the guilt

. . .

Yeah. I knew that anyway, it was secondhand, I knew it.

Well dont give us any crap then man if that's what ye're giving us.

I'm no.

Well dont.

Where the fucking hell is he anyway?

I dont know man, he never tells me nothing, bastard.

The Later Transgression

At this stage, when things appeared to be running smoothly, his transgression surprised me. Upon reflection it was no more and no less than I should have anticipated. His life may have been seen as one to emulate, to strive after or towards, but it was far from commendable. I knew that. He had not lived a perfect life. My friends respected him; young men like ourselves. It is safe to say that.

A companion of ours, a musician, did not survive though his existence exhausted itself in a similar way. When we three were together and smiling on how things had been, partly it was relief that we had survived at all. None among us pretended, none among us was the hypocrite.

In the ordinary ethical sense we had not lived just lives but nor had we pretensions towards the religious or theological sense of other existences, nor of existences yet to come. For myself I had no intentions of accepting a second existence. I grew weary of Lives to Come, a Life to Come, that Life to Come. As with our former friend I was one of many, content that those who follow should wield the baton.

Universals do not exist. There is no ethic, no code of morality, no moral sense at the inner depth of our being.

From an early period I too was aware that the sensibility is unaffected by the violence or abuses perpetrated by one on another, even if the one is close to us. Yet I was perceived as ruthless. So too was our former friend. But did he fully understand what ruthlessness might amount to? Perhaps he did. When his grandfather died he rowed the boat that carried his ashes. His father and younger brother were seated at the stern. His younger brother unscrewed the receptacle and emptied the ashes midway across. His father could have stopped him. The following is hearsay, that he too could have stopped him.

learning the Story

I once met an old lady sitting under a bridge over the River Kelvin. She smoked Capstan full-strength cigarettes and played the mouthorgan.

The moon was well up as I had passed along the footpath listening to the water fall at the small dam beyond the old mill. Aye, cried the voice, you are there are you! If I had spotted her before she had me I would have crept back the way I had come. Aye, she cried again. And rising to her feet she brought out the mouthorgan from somewhere inside the layers of her clothing, and struck up the tune: Maxwelton Braes Are Bonny was the name of it. Halfway through she suddenly stopped and she stared at me and grunted something. She sat down again on the damp grass with her back against the wall at the tunnel entrance; she stared at her boots. Very good that, I said to her. From her shopping bag she pulled out the packet of Capstan full-strength cigarettes. She sniffed. And I felt as if I had let her down. I always liked that tune, I told her. She struck a match and lighted a cigarette. She flicked the match a distance and it landed with smoke still rising from it. Drawing the shopping bag in between her raised knees she inhaled deeply, exhaled staring at her boots. Cheerio then, I said. I paced on beneath the bridge aware of my footsteps echoing.

The old lady wore specs and had a scarf wrapped round her neck. Her nose was bony. Her skirt may have showed under the hem of her coat. When she was playing the mouthorgan she had moved slightly from foot to foot. Her coat was furry.

Manchester in July

I was there once without enough for a room, not even for a night's lodgings in the local Walton House. 6/6d it was at the time which proves how fucking recent it was. At the NAB a clerk proffered a few bob as a temporary measure and told me to come back once I had fixed myself up with a rentbook. I got irritated at this because of the logical absurdity but they were not obliged to dish out cash to people without addresses. By the time I had worked out my anger I was skint again (10 fags and some sort of basic takeaway from a Chinese Restaurant). I wound up trying for a kip in the station, then tramped about the 'dilly trying to punt the wares to Mr and Mrs Anybody. When it was morning I headed along and under the bridge to Salford, eventually picking up another few bob in the office across from Strangeways. I went away back there and then and booked in at the Walton for that coming evening, just to be on the safe side.

The middle of July. What a wonderful heat it was. I spent most of the day snoozing full stretch on my back in a grass square adjacent to the House, doing my best to conserve the rest of the bread.

Into the communal lounge about 6.30 p.m. I sat on this ancient leather effort of a chair which had brass studs stuck in it. The other seating in the place was similarly odd and disjointed. Old guys sprawled everywhere snoring and farting and burping and staring in a glassy-eyed way at the television. I had been scratching myself as soon as I crossed the threshold, just at the actual idea of it. Yet in a funny fucking way it was quite comfortable and relaxing and it seemed to induce in you a sort of stupor. Plus it was fine getting the chance to see a telly again. One felt like a human being. I mind it was showing The Fugitive with that guy David Jansen and this tall police lieutenant who was chasing him about the States (and wound up he was the guy who killed Jansen's wife). I was right into it anyway, along with the remaining few in the room who were still compos mentis, when in walks these three blokes in clean boilersuits and they switched it off, the telly. 10 minutes before the end or something. I jumped out the chair and stood there glaring at them. A couple of the old guys got up then; but they just headed off towards the door, and then upstairs to the palliases. It was fucking bedtime! 10.50 p.m. on a Thursday night. It might even have been a fucking Friday.

The Habits of Rats

This part of the factory had always been full of rats. It was the storeroom. Large piles of boxes were stacked at the bottom end while scattered about the floor was all manner of junk. Here in particular dwelled the rats. They came out at night. During the nightshift one man had charge of the storeroom; he was always pleased when somebody called up with an order and stayed for a chat. His office lay at the opposite end of the storeroom. He would keep all the lights on here but leave the bottom end in darkness, unless being obliged to go down to collect a box from stock, in which case he switched on every light in the entire place to advise the rats of his approach.

One night a gaffer phoned him on the intercom and told him to get such and such a box and deliver it immediately to the machineshop. Now the storeman had been halfway through the first of his cheese sandwiches at the time but the interruption did not annoy him. There was little work to keep his mind occupied during the night; he was always glad of the opportunity to wander round the factory pushing his wheelbarrow.

Once he had all the lights on at the bottom end he found himself to be holding his parcel of cheese sandwiches. Stuffing the remainder of the one he had been eating straight into his mouth he laid the parcel down on a box so that he could manoeuvre the requisitioned box onto the wheelbarrow. He pushed it along to the exit. He switched off the lights as he went. Outside the storeroom he halted. He dashed back inside and switched them on again and quickly went down to retrieve the sandwiches before the rats could gobble them all up. In his office he placed the parcel on top of a filing cabinet.

He enjoyed the wander, stopping off here and there for a smoke or a chat with particular people he was friendly with. Back in the storeroom he brewed a fresh pot of tea and sat down to continue his lunchbreak. He only ate two of the sandwiches.

Later on in the night a gaffer phoned him with another requisition. He phoned back after when again there was no reply. Eventually he came round in person, to discover the storeman lying on the floor in a coma. He had the storeman rushed off to hospital at once.

For a fortnight the storeman remained in this coma. They took out all of his blood and filled him up with other blood. They said that a rat, or rats, had urinated on his sandwiches and thus had his entire blood system been poisoned.

The storeman said he could remember a slight dampness about the sandwiches he had eaten, but that they had definitely not been soggy. He reckoned the warmth of his office may have dried them out a bit. He said when he left them lying on the box he must have forgotten to close the parcel properly. But he was only gone moments. He could not understand it at all. After his period of convalescence they transferred him to a permanent job on the dayshift, across in the machineshop.

The Melveille Twins, page 82

The long feud between the Melveille Twins was resolved by a duel in which stipulations of rather obvious significance had been laid down, the two men were bound back to back by a length of thick hemp knotted round their waists. Having gained choice of weapon the elder had already decided upon the cutlass and insofar as the younger is noted as having been 'corrie-fistit',[1] to infer a hint of possible irony may not be misguided. Few events of a more bloodthirsty nature are thought to have occasioned in the country of Scotland.

When the handkerchief fell the slashing began; within moments the lower part of each body was running red with blood. While wielding the weapon each held the empty hand aloft as though unwilling so much as to even touch the other. Eventually the small group of men silently observing, made their way off from the scene – a scene that for them had soon proved sour.

Only one man remained. He seems to have been a servant of some sort but little is known of his history aside from the fact of his being fairly literate.

The affair appeared at an end when the elder twin

---

[1] To be 'corrie-fistit' in certain parts of Scotland is to be left-handed, even in the present day.

stumbled and together they landed on the ground. But almost immediately each had rolled in such a manner they were lying on the hands that grasped the weapons: for a brief period they kicked at each other. Coming to them with a jug of fresh water and strips of a clean material, the man bathed their wounds. He then lifted and placed the weapons outwith their arms' reach; he departed at this point. Whether the actual duel ended here is an open question. We are only certain that the feud ceased.

le jouer

Him with the long face and that conical hat sitting there with the clay pipe stuck in his mouth, the widower: he enters this café around 7 every evening with a nod to the barman, a quick look to ensure his chair and table are vacant; though in a place as quiet as this anything else seems out of the question. Lurking about at the rear of the table is a wee black & white dog that finally settles into a prone position in the shadows by the wall beneath the grimy mirror. On putting the tall bottle of wine and the two glasses down onto the table, the widower has tugged this huge coloured handkerchief from his right jacket pocket, and into it has given a muffled honk; and sniffed while stuffing it back out of sight. Several moments on he is glancing across at the clock on the gantry and taking the handkerchief out once more, to wipe at his nostrils.

The door has opened.

That younger man – him with the upturned brim on his hat – has walked in, hands in coat pockets; and a half twitch of the head by way of greeting the barman; and a half rise of the eyebrows on seeing the widower's glance at the clock. A deck of cards he lifts from the bar en route to the empty seat facing the widower. With a slow yawn the dog lowers its head, closes its eyes, reverting into its prone position. While the wine is being poured by one the other is shuffling to deal methodically, ten cards apiece.

Later, him with the conical hat will rise and knock the bowl of the clay pipe against the heel of his right boot and without so much as a grunt will head for the exit followed by the wee black & white dog; and this dog must dodge smartly to get out before the door shuts on it.

That younger man will have refilled his own glass and will then gather up the cards and, as he is shuffling, he will be gazing round the interior of the room: but the only person present apart from the barman will be Paul Cézanne: and so he will continue to shuffle the cards for a period, before setting out the first game of solitaire while half wondering if his kids are behaving themselves.

not too long from now tonight
/will be that last time

He was walking slowly. His pace quickened then slackened once more. He stopped by the doorway of a shop and lighted a cigarette. The floor was dry, a sort of parquetry. He lowered himself down to sit on his heels, his arms folded, elbows resting on his knees, his back to the glass door.

He could have gone straight home and crept inside and into bed perhaps quietly enough not to disturb her and come morning, maybe that hour earlier than usual, and out and away, before she was awake. But why bother. He could simply not return. In this way they would simply not meet, they would not have to meet. And that would be great. He was not up to it. It was not something he felt capable of managing. It was not something he was capable of. He could not cope with it.

But why bother. If he was obliged to do certain things and then failed to do these things then that was that and nothing could be offered instead. He had always known the truth of that. Always; even though he seemed never to have given it voice. Never; especially not with her. She would never have understood.

And then there were his silences. That inability he had to get out of himself. It was not disgust, not contempt; nothing like that. It was something different altogether. But he had no wish to work out what the hell it was.

He had been trying to adapt for years. And now she was there now lying in bed sleeping or awake, about to become awake, to peer at the clockface, knowing she is not as warm as usual, because of course he is not home yet and the time, and her eyes.

He keeps imagining going somewhere else and taking a room perhaps with full board in some place far away where all the people are just people, people he does not know and has no obligation to speak to. There was something good about that. He inhaled on the cigarette then raised himself up and bent his knees a couple of times, before pacing on. After a time he slowed, but was soon walking more quickly.

Roofsliding[2]

The tenement building upon which the practice occurs is of the three storey variety. A section of roof bounded on both sides by a row of chimney stacks is favoured. No reason is known as to why this particular section should be preferred to another. Certain members of the group participating are thought to reside outwith this actual building though none is a stranger to the district. Roofsliding, as it is termed, can take place more than once per week and will always do so during a weekday mid-morning. As to the season of the year, this is unimportant; dry days, however, being much sought after.

The men arise in single file from out of the rectangular skylight. They walk along the peak of the roof ensuring that one foot is settling on either side of the jointure which is bevelled in design, the angle at the peak representing some 80 degrees. During the walk slates have been known to break loose from their fixtures and if bypassing the gutter will topple over the edge of the building to land on the pavement far below. To offset

---

[2] This account has been taken more or less verbatim from a pamphlet entitled *Within Our City Slums*; it belongs to the chapter headed 'Curious practices of the Glaswegian'. The pamphlet was published in 1932 but is still available in a few secondhand bookshops in the south of England.

any danger to the public a boy can always be seen on the opposite pavement, from where he will give warning to the pedestrians.

When the men, sometime designated roofsliders, have assembled along the peak they will lower themselves to a sitting posture on the jointure, the legs being outstretched flatly upon the sloped roof. They face to the front of the building. Roofsliding will now commence. The feet push forward until the posterior moves off from the jointure onto the roof itself, the process continuing until the body as a whole lies prone on the gradient at which point momentum is effected.

Whether a man 'slides' with arms firmly aligned to the trunk, or akimbo, or indeed lying loosely to the sides, would appear to be a function of the number of individuals engaged in the activity at any given period (as many as 32 are said to have participated on occasion). Legs are, however, kept tightly shut. When the feet come to rest on the gutter roofsliding halts at once and the order in which members finish plays no part in the practice.

A due pause will now occur. Afterwards the men manoeuvre themselves inch by inch along the edge of the roof while yet seeming to maintain the prone position. Their goal, the line of chimney stacks that stand up right to the northside of the section. From here the men make their way up to the jointure on hands and knees. It is worth noting that they do so by way of the outside, unwilling, it would appear, to hazard even the slightest damage to the 'sliding' section that is bounded between here and the line of chimney stacks to the southside. When all have gathered on the jointure once again they will be seated to face the rear of the building. Now and now only shall conversation be entered upon. For up until this period not a man amongst them shall have spoken (since arrival by way of the skylight).

At present a ruddy-complexioned chap in his 44th year is the 'elder statesman' of the roofsliders. Although the ages do vary within the group no youth shall be admitted who has yet to attain his 14th birthday. On the question of alcohol members are rightly severe, for not only would the 'wrong doer' be at mortal risk, so too would the lives of each individual.

As a phenomenon there can be no doubt as to the curious nature of the practice of roofsliding. Further observation might well yield fruits.

Busted Scotch

I had been looking forward to this Friday night for a while. The first wage from the first job in England. The workmates had assured me they played Brag in this club's casino. It would start when the cabaret ended. Packed full of bodies inside the main hall; rows and rows of men-only drinking pints of bitter and yelling at the strippers. One of the filler acts turned out to be a scotchman doing this harrylauder thing complete with kilt and trimmings. A terrible disgrace. Keep Right On To The End Of The Road he sang with four hundred and fifty males screaming Get Them Off Jock. Fine if I had been drunk and able to join in on the chants but as it was I was staying sober for the Brag ahead. Give the scotchman his due but – he stuck it out till the last and turning his back on them all he gave a big boo boopsidoo with the kilt pulled right up and flashing the Y-fronts. Big applause he got as well. The next act on was an Indian Squaw. Later I saw the side door into the casino section opening. I went through. Blackjack was the game until the cabaret finished. I sat down facing a girl around my own age, she was wearing a black dress cut off the shoulders. Apart from me there was no other punters in the room.

Want to start, she asked.

Aye. Might as well. I took out my wages.

O, you're scotch. One of your countrymen was on stage tonight.

That a fact.

She nodded as she prepared to deal. She said, How much are you wanting to bet?

I shrugged. I pointed to the wages lying there on the edge of the baize.

All of it . . .

Aye. The lot.

She covered the bet after counting what I had. She dealt the cards.

Twist.

Bust . . .

A Rolling Machine

Sandy had been leading me around all morning in a desire to impress – to interest me in him and in this place where he earned his living, also to show his workmates that here he was with his very own learner. He explained various workings and techniques of the machines and asked if I had any queries but not to worry if I didnt because at this stage it was unlikely though I would soon become familiar with it all, just so long as I took it easy and watched everything closely. Gradually he was building to the climax of his own machine. Here I was to learn initially. Up and down he strode patting its parts and referring to it as her and she as if it was a bus or an old-fashioned sailing ship. She wont let you down Jimmy is the sort of stuff he was giving me. The machine was approximately twenty-five feet in length and was always requiring attention from the black squad; but even so, it could produce the finest quality goods of the entire department when running to her true form. Placing me to the side in such a way that I could have an unrestricted view he kicked her off. He was trying hard not to look too pleased with himself. Every now and then he shifted stance to ensure I was studying his movements. His foot was going on the pedal while his right hand was holding the wooden peg-like instrument through which he played the coiled wire between the middle and forefingers of his left hand out onto the rolling section of the apparatus. At one point he turned to make a comment but a knot had appeared on the wire, jamming on the wooden instrument and ripping off the top end of his thumb while the machine continued the rolling operation and out of the fleshy mess spiralled a hair-thin substance like thread being unrolled from a bobbin somewhere inside the palm, and it was running parallel to the wire from the coil. Sandy's eyes were gazing at me in a kind of astonished embarrassment until eventually he collapsed, just a moment before one of his workmates elbowed me clear in order to reach the trip-safety-rail.

Even Money

It was a bit strange to see the two of them. She was
wee and skinny with a really pecked-out crabbit face.
He was also skinny, but shifty looking. Difficult to tell
why he was shifty looking. Maybe he wasnt. Aye he was,
he was fucking shifty looking and that's final. He was
following her. He could easily have caught up with her
and introduced hisself but he didnt, he just followed her,
in steady pursuit, at a safe distance. And that is the action
of a shifty character. The fact that a well-thumbed copy
of the Sporting Life poked out from his coat pocket is
neither here nor there. Being a betting man myself I've
always resented the shady associations punters have for
non-bettors. Anyhow, back to the story, the distance
between the pair amounted to twenty yards, and there is
an interesting point to discuss. It is this: the wee woman
actually passed the man in the first place and may have
seen him. She could have nodded or even spoken to him.
But she did seem not to notice him. Because of that I
dont know whether she knew him or not. And it is not
possible to say if he knew her. He looked to be following
her in an off-hand kind of fashion. When she stopped
outside the post office he paused. In she went. But just as
you were thinking, Aw aye, there he goes . . . Naw; he
didnt, he just walked on.

Samaritans

Heh man what d'you make of this like I mean I'm standing in the betting shop and this guy comes over. Heh john, he says, you got a smoke?

A smoke . . .

Aye, he says.

So okay I mean you dont like to see a cunt without a smoke. Okay, I says, here.

Ta.

Puts it in his mouth while I'm clawing myself to find a match.

Naw, he's saying, I dont like going to the begging games . . .

Fair enough, I says, I've been skint myself.

Aw it's no that, he says, I'm no skint.

And out comes this gold lighter man and he flicks it and that and the flame, straight away, no bother. Puffs out the smoke. I'm waiting for the bank to open at half one, he says, I've got a cheque to cash.

Good, I says, but I'm thinking well fuck you as well, that's my last fag man I mean jesus christ almighty.

Foreign language users

A wise man resists playing cards with foreign language users. This is a maxim Mister Joseph Kerr should always have been well aware of. So how come he had succumbed to temptation yet again? Because he thought he would take them, that's how. If you had discussed the point prior to play he would have nodded in a perfunctory fashion – that's how much a part of him the maxim was. And yet he still succumbed. Of course. Gamblers are a strange breed. In fact, when he noticed his pockets were empty he frowned. That is exactly what he did, he frowned. Then he stared at the foreign language users who by this time had forgotten all about him. And the croupier was shuffling the deck for a new deal. And yes, she was also concealing her impatience in an unsubtle way, this croupier, and this unsubtlety was her method of displaying it, her impatience.

Mister Joseph Kerr nudged the spectacles up his nose a wee bit, a nervous gesture. His chair moved noisily, causing the other players to glance at him.

But what was he to do now? There was nothing he could do now. No, nothing to be done. It was something he just had to face. And yet these damn foreign language users had taken his money by devices one could scarcely describe as being other than less than fair, not to put too fine a point on things. And how in the name of all that's holy could the fact that it was himself to blame be of any consolation?

He scratched his ear and continued to stand there, by the chair, and then he sighed in an exaggerated manner but it was bitterly done, and he declared how things had gone too far for him now, that he had so to speak come to the end of his tether. The croupier merely looked at him in reply but this look might well have been a straightforward appeal for a new player.

Mister Joseph Kerr shrugged. Then he stood to the side, making space for the new player who moved easily onto the seat. There was a pause. Mister Joseph Kerr had raised his eyebrows in a slightly mocking fashion. He smiled at the new player and touched him on the shoulder, saying how he should definitely pay heed to that which he knew so thoroughly beforehand. The new player glared at the hand on his shoulder. What's the meaning of this? he murmured.

In all probability he too was a foreign language user. Mister Joseph Kerr nodded wearily. Maybe he was just bloody well growing old! Could that be it? He sighed as he strolled round the table, continuing on in the style of somebody heading to an exit. He entered the gents' washroom and gazed at himself in the mirror. It was a poor show right enough, this tired face he saw; and something in it too as if, as if his eyes had perhaps clouded over, but his spectacles of course, having misted over. The thought how at least he was breathing, at least he was breathing, that was worth remembering.

Good Intentions

We had been sceptical from the very outset but the way he set about the tasks suited us perfectly. In fact, it was an eye-opener. He would stand there with the poised rifle, the weather-beaten countenance, the shiny little uniform; yet giving absolutely nothing away. His legs were bandy and it produced a swaggering stance, as though he had no time for us and deep down regarded us as amateurs. But we, of course, made no comment. The old age pensioner is a strange beast on occasion and we were well acquainted with this, perhaps too well acquainted. In the final analysis it was probably that at the root of the project's failure.

This man for fuck sake

This man for fuck sake it was terrible seeing him walk down the edge of the pavement. If he'd wanted litter we would've given him it. The trouble is we didn't know it at the time. So all we could do was watch his progress and infer. And even under normal circumstances this is never satisfactory: it has to be readily understood the types of difficulty we laboured under. Then that rolling manoeuvre he performed while nearing the points of reference. It all looked to be going so fucking straightforward. How can you blame us? You can't, you can't fucking blame us.

Half an hour before he died

About half an hour before he died Mr Millar woke up, aware that he might start seeing things from out the different shapes in the bedroom, especially all these clothes hanging on the pegs on the door, their suddenly being transformed into ghastly kinds of bodies, perhaps hovering in mid air. It was not a good feeling; and having reflected on it for quite a few minutes he began dragging himself up onto his elbows to peer about the place. And his wrists felt really strange, as if they were bloodless or something, bereft of blood maybe, no blood at all to course through the veins. For a wee while he became convinced he was losing his sanity altogether, but no, it was not that, not that precisely; what it was, he saw another possibility, and it was to do with crossing the edge into a sort of madness he had to describe as 'proper' – a proper madness. And as soon as he recognized the distinction he began to feel better, definitely. Then came the crashing of a big lorry, articulated by the sound of it. Yes, it always had been a liability this, living right on top of such a busy bloody road. He was resting on his elbows still, considering all of it, how it had been so noisy, at all hours of the day and night. Terrible. He felt like shouting on the wife to come ben so's he could tell her about it, about how he felt about it, but he was feeling far too tired and he had to lie back down.

The Principal's Decision

The Principal here was known to have hesitated before lifting the dishcloth which he used to wipe clean the blood. I did not witness the hesitation. It was reported. When he had wiped clean the blood he glanced to where I was standing by the door. I was his associate and waited there. The body lay crumpled in its own heap. This was approved. The Principal reached towards it but only for purposes of evaluation. He was not being observed, not as such. But I saw that his eyes closed. This part of the practice is found wearisome by some. In those days I supposed that its continued existence was for decorative purposes but I took part in it. My interest was genuine. It had occurred to me that if decoration had no part in the practice then aspects of it were mere obsession. Allowing for this, if it were a form of obsession might the Principal have employed it for decorative purposes? If so I thought it admirable. I have to say that I did. At the age I then was it brought a smile to my face. It later occurred to me that he wished to be rid of it altogether, signified by the hesitation before lifting the dishcloth.

Music in the background. A nocturne by Henry Rocastle sent the Principal into a dreamy condition. Art was his passion, or so he maintained.

Would he wait until it finished? No, not him. He used his foot to manoeuvre the ruffled edge of the corpse's clothes. The untidiness made him grue. Yet his facility to operate in the most trying circumstances, withal, was here to the fore when he could never have stopped himself reaching downwards, and seemed to notice his own fingers curl in preparation. Whether he approved or not I could not say.

He had a degree of self-consciousness that I knew to respect. I watched how he sighed yet easily lifted the corpse's arm, let it fall. The arbitrary action might have made it the more natural, removing a general untidiness, so to speak. But this untidiness could not be removed from himself, not altogether. Arthritis would have him cornered in not many years hence. This was reported to me. By then I had advanced in a manner that demanded he be placed on retreat.

The Principal's very professionalism allowed the distance between truth and appearance. It is not enough to state that I respected this quality. I was experienced in the field but not expert. Whether this was enough to secure the primary position time alone would tell. I saw that the elbow of the corpse had bended. Should this have been corrected? Queries of this form can be posed objectively. Workable inferences may be ascertained by examination of the interior.

A course of potential activity, from either or both, is safely predicted. Patience did not enter into these proceedings. He expected objectivity if not indifference. Either was a reward, having its own significance.

The arrangement of articles displayed on the shelving inclined towards order, irrelevant to the overall picture which was already contained in the above. Severing a limb was pointless. Such a possibility had presented itself. The result would exist as inconsistent. The Principal would not accept such. The result would further illustrate a pattern. The pattern would appear perfect, after its own fashion. Perfection of this type is not what is required. Thus the Principal looked to myself. I knew this as a ruse. I glanced at the large wall-clock. His decision belonged to an earlier generation. In these harsher times alternative courses of action were hypothetical. This was the nature of the Principality. On another occasion, and in less immediate circumstances, I might have smiled. The next time he glimpsed the clock it would have stopped altogether. Not through any action of his. Such would never happen. He would look to me. Any decision of mine required due process. I might have smiled. My pulse had quickened and I wet my lips. The proper matter I should have happen is what would happen and what must happen, and in the correct time, but to no avail.

The Principal studied me. I knew reality and hoped that a truth lay between us. Nevertheless I departed the room. I strode into the adjacent room. I then witnessed the Principal stand alone. There would be no private smile. It was as it was and his practice dictated a practice. It was nothing to him. Personal detail is of no account in situations of this nature. Our work concerns extensions, parts and bodies. The Principal peers at the corpse, now comfortable in its presence. He could have filled a kettle, made and poured a cup of tea. Such moves enabled promotion and were victories. Their nature would enable my own promotion. It was no thanks to know that his had depended on my absence, but perhaps not.

That Thread

After the pause came the other pause and it was the way they have of following each other the next one already in its place as if the sequence was arranged according to some design or other, and set not just by the first but them all, a networked silence. It was that way when she entered the room. The noise having ceased right enough but even allowing for that if it hadnt it would have – which is usually always the case. She had the looks to attract, a figure exactly so, her sensuousness in all the moves so that her being there in this objectified way, the sense of a thousand eyes. Enter softly enter softly: it was like a song he was singing, and her smile brief, yet bravado as well, that style some women have especially, the face, the self-consciousness; and all of them being there and confronting her while her just there taking it, standing there, one arm down, her fingers bent, brushing the hem of her skirt. She was not worried by virtue of him, the darkness of the room, any of it. Like a sure knowledge of her own disinterest, his non-existence as a sexual being, in relation to her, and he grinned, reaching for the whisky and pouring himself one, adding a half again of water, the whisky not being a good one. She was still standing there, as if dubiously. She was seeking out faces she recognised and his was one that she did recognise, lo, but would barely acknowledge, she would never acknowledge. Had he been the only face to recognise; the only one. Even that. He smiled then the sudden shift out from his side jacket pocket with the lighter and snap, the flare in the gloom, the thin exhalation of blue smoke; he sipped at the whisky and water, for his face would definitely have had to be recognised now, from the activity, no matter how softly, softly and quietly, no matter how he had contrived it. Now his elation was so fucking strong, so fucking vivid man, and striking, and so entirely fucking wonderful he wanted to scream he had to scream he really did have to he had to scream he would have to he wouldnt be able to fucking stop himself he was shaking he was shaking the cuff of his sleeve, the cuff of his sleeve, trailing on the surface of the table, his hand shaking, shaking, now twitching and his breath coming deep, and she would have sensed it, sensed it all, and she would be smiling so slightly around the corners of her mouth, the down there, her thick lower lip how round it was, how round it was and mystifying, to describe it as provocative was an actual error, an error, a mistake. But the hesitancy in her movement. That thread having been long flung out now, though still exploratory, but ensnaring, it was ensnaring, causing her to hold there, so unmistakably hesitant now rubbing her shoulder just so self-aware yet in that kind of fashion a woman has of rubbing her shoulder at the slightest sensory indication of the thread, feeling it cling, that quiver and he shivered, raising the whisky to his mouth and sipping it, keeping his elbow hard in to the side of his body, keeping it firmly there because that sickness in the pit of his belly and the blood coursing through his cheeks, and burning, burning, everyone seeing and knowing, he was so transparent, so transparent, she just shook her head. What was she going to do? She just had shaken her head that most brief way, and she turned on her heel and she left, left him there. He couldnt move. He would cry out. But his face was controlled, so controlled, although the colour now drained from his cheeks, or else the opposite, was it the opposite? and his hand now shaking, the cigarette lighter on the coffee table.

Sarah Crosbie

The big house was standing empty for years before she came back. She came from America. But according to the newspaperman she had owned the house long long before. The big house stood at the end of the street, less than a hundred yards from the river. There was not much the people in the street could tell him. The old woman never spoke to them at all. She had always lived alone surrounded by cats and dogs. *Sarah Crosbie*. It turned out that the house had been there about two hundred years. This bit of the river had been a ford at one time. The foundations were much older than the rest of the building. Somebody called Rankine had rebuilt it and the date 1733 was discovered above a side door at the back. This Rankine was famous. The newspaperman was looking for people called Rankine to see if they were related. He thought the old woman might have been a descendant. But nobody knew. People kept away from the big house. If a neighbour or somebody ever had to go to her door she always kept them waiting on the front step. When the McDonnell Murders were going on back in the '20s a group of locals barged their way inside the big house door. They found a body behind a bricked-up chimney-piece down in the basement. A man's body, dead for many years. Nobody knew a thing about it and neither did the old woman. She had not been in the place long at the time. The police thought he might have died from natural causes and judging by the tatters of clothes he could have been a building worker or something.

When she went into hospital the newspaperman tried to gain entrance to the big house but he was refused on certain grounds. Workmen arrived the next day and they barred the place up.

It was eighteen months ago she turned up at the police office. She was in a bad state. She told them people were in her house, they had done things to her. But she would not say what things. Policemen returned to the big house with her but saw nothing suspicious. Next day a health-visitor called on her and she was admitted later on to the geriatric ward at Gartnavel Royal. A few women from the street took a bunch of flowers up to her but she just stared at the ceiling for the whole visiting hour. And it was after this the newspaperman began coming around. He goes to see her in hospital as well once or twice.

the Hon

Auld Shug gits oot iv bed. Turns aff the alarm cloak. Gis straight ben the toilit. Sits doon in that oan the lavatri pan. Wee bit iv time gis by. Shug sittin ther, yonin. This Hon. Up it comes oot fri the waste pipe. Stretchis right up. Grabs him by the bolls.

Jesis christ shouts the Shug filla.

The Hon gis slack in a coupla minits. Up jumps Shug. Straight ben the kitchin hodin onti the pyjama troosirs in that jist aboot collapsin inti his cher.

Never know the minit he was sayin. Eh. Jesis christ.

Looks up at the cloak oan the mantelpiece. Eftir seven. Time he was away tae his work. Couldni move bit. Shatird. Jist sits ther in the cher.

Fuck it he says Am no gon.

Coupla oors gis by. In comes the wife an that ti stick oan a kettle. Sees the auld yin sittin ther. Well past time. Day's wages oot the windi.

Goodnis sake Shug she shouts yir offi late.

Pokes him in the chist. Kneels doon oan the fler. He isni movin. Nay signs a taw. Pokes him ance mer. Still nothin bit. Then she sees he's deid. Faints. Right nix ti the Shug filla's feet. Lyin ther. The two iv them. Wan in the cher in wan in the fler. A hof oor later a chap it the door. Nay answer. Nother chap. Sound iv a key in the door. Door shuts. In comes the lassie. Eywis comes roon fir a blether wi the maw in that whin the auld yin's oot it his work. Merrit hersel. Man's a bad yin but. Cunt's never worked a day in his life. Six weans tay. Whin she sees thim ther she twigs right away.

My goad she shouts thir deid. Ma maw in ma da ir deid.

She bends doon ti make sure.

O thank goad she says ma maw's jist faintit. Bit da. Da's deid. O naw. Ma da's deid, Goad love us.

That Other

The people filed into the Memorial Tower in some consternation for the culprit was still at the gate, still shrieking that horrific blasphemy.

And all the while the foolish inconsistency prevailed.

Of those involved only two individuals could even hope to be aware of its singular significance. Yet the people were now spiralling upwards, blinking.

More complaints from the American Correspondent

Jesus Christ man this tramping from city to city – terrible. No pavements man just these back gardens like you got to walk right down by the edge of the road man and them big fucking doberman pinschers they're coming charging straight at you. Then the ghettos for christ sake you got all them mothers lining the streets man they're tugging at your sleeves, hey you, gies a bite of your cheeseburger. Murder polis.

The guy with the crutch

A gangrenous patch on his right leg had resulted in amputation. The people at the hospital gave him a new one which he got used to quicker than most folk in the same predicament but something happened to this new limb and now he no longer had it. For a while he moved around as best he could, making do with a walking stick of sorts; but it was not easy and he was a guy who liked travelling about the place. One morning somebody found a broken crutch and gave him it and somebody else made a cross-spar and nailed it properly down for him. This meant he was back mobile again and he used to tell folk the crutch was as adequate as anything. But eventually he stopped telling them that and soon he stopped telling them anything at all. From then on, whenever I caught sight of him, he was carrying a plastic shopper that contained most of his possessions; usually he was trudging to places over stretches of waste ground, although trudging is the wrong word because of having the crutch and so on he used to move in a rigorous and quite quick swinging motion.

undeciphered tremors

In the ensuing scramble the body will melt into undeciphered tremors, undeciphered in consequence of its having been laid to rest some time prior to the call. And the 'call' here must not be regarded as figurative; it will have proceeded from whence great difficulty is experienced in matters of prediction. You must also recall the state of non well-being which exists beforehand. It is certainly the case that one has to exercise caution in hazarding a judgment but nevertheless, nevertheless, I would say if you feel the need to leap then by all means leap.

Incident on a Windswept Beach

A man walked out of the sea one February morning dressed in a boilersuit & bunnet, and wearing a tartan scarf which had been tucked crosswise under each oxter to be fastened by a safety-pin at a point roughly centre of his shoulder blades; from his neck swung a pair of heavy boots whose laces were knotted together. He brought what must have been a waterproof tobacco-pouch out from a pocket, because when he had rolled a smoke he lighted the thing using a kind of Zippo (also from the pouch) and puffed upon it with an obvious relish. It was an astonishing spectacle.

Hastening over to him I exclaimed: Christ Almighty jimmy, where've you come from?

Back there, he muttered oddly and made to proceed on his path.

At least let me give you a pair of socks! I said.

But he shook his head. No . . . I'm not supposed to.

Being Lifted, how it was

I shrugged. People wonder if something bad might have happened. They begin thinking that. They dont see you around and fear the worst. That is what happened to me. People wondered and I could not blame them.

Were you wondering that when they lifted you?

Being honest, I suppose I did. You're probably talking the first time.

Yeah.

That was when they came to the house. The second time they didn't care, broad daylight in the street. The kids were coming out of school. I was waiting for my two.

Your children?

Yes.

They did it in front of your children?

I smiled. This is real life remember, not television.

What did ye think?

When?

When it happened?

I didn't think fuck all. Nothing. No really. Maybe at the back of my mind. I might have been thinking something. Maybe that she wanted a break or what; they have a word for it, before a divorce. What do they call it again? Mutual consent, mutual parting or something like maybe she just wanted out for a wee while. That happens with relationships, ye need a breather; sometimes ye do. Maybe she went to see her weans, her own weans. I dont know. Christ she might even have telt me. And I forgot.

Many weans has she got?

Two. Plus the two with me. She's married. No to me, another cunt. I got up from the chair. Want a cup of tea?

No, sorry. Well I would, but

Nay bother.

I have to be back in the office.

Sure.

The Failure

Whereas the drop appeared to recede into black nothingness I deduced each side of the chasm to taper until they merged. Each falling object would eventually land. And if footholes were to exist then discovering them could scarcely be avoided. The black of the nothingness was only so from the top: light would be perceived at the bottom, a position from where even the tiniest of specks would enable the black to be quashed. And should a problem arise, groping an ascent via the footholes would be fairly certain.

I jumped.

The sensation of the fall is indescribable.

Much later upon landing I faced black nothingness. I had been mistaken about the light. That speck was insufficient. I could distinguish nothing whatsoever. But it was impossible to concentrate for my boots were wedged into the sides and my knees were twisted unnaturally. My arms had been forced round onto my back, with my shoulders pressed forward. The entire position of my body was reminiscent of what the adept yogi may accomplish. I ached all over. Then I had become aware of how irresponsibly conceived my planning had been. It was as if somehow I had expected the bottom to be large enough to accommodate an average-sized, fully grown male.

For a lengthy period I attempted to dislodge myself but to no avail. I panicked. I clawed and clawed at the backs of my thighs in an effort to hoist up my legs until finally I was obliged to halt through sheer fatigue at the wrists and finger-joints. Sweat dripped from my every pore; and the echo consequent upon this was resounding. Beginning from the drips the noise developed into one continuous roar that increased as it rose and rose and rose before dying away out of the top. An awful realization was presenting itself to me: the more I tried and tried to dislodge my body the more firmly entrenched I would become. Think of the manner whereby a mouse seals its own fate within that most iniquitous of adhesives it has entered to search out that last scrap of food. Yes, an immediate reaction to a desperate situation may well be normal but it is rarely other than misguided. My own had resulted in a position of utter hopelessness. And the magnitude of my miscalculations seemed destined to overwhelm me. That failure to anticipate the absurdity of bottom.

No, not a mouse, nor yet a flea, could enter into that. Total nothingness. A space so minute only nothing gains entry. Not even the most supremely infinitesimal of organisms as witnessed through the finest of powerful microscopes can disturb the bottom, for here absolutely nothing exists but the point in itself, the vertex.

An old story

She had been going about in this depressed state for ages so I should have known something was up. But I didnt. You dont always see what's in front of your nose. I've been sitting about the house that long. You wind up in a daze. You dont see things properly, even with the weans, the weans especially. There again but she's no a wean. No now. She's a young woman. Ach, I dont want to tell this story.

But you cant say that. Obviously the story has to get told.

Mm, aye, I know what you mean.

Fine then.

Mmm.

Okay, so about your story . . .

Aye.

It concerns a lassie, right? And she's in this depressed state, because of her boyfriend probably – eh?

I dont want to tell it.

But you've got to tell it. You've got to tell it. Unless . . . if it's no really a story at all.

Oh aye christ it's a story, dont worry about that.

Getting Outside

I'll tell you something: when I stepped outside that door I was alone, and I mean alone. And it was exactly what I had wanted, almost as if I'd been demanding it. And that was funny because it's not the kind of thing I would usually demand at all; usually I didnt demand anything remotely resembling being outside that door. But now. Christ. And another thing: I didnt even feel as if I was myself. What a bloody carry on it was. I stared down at my legs, at my trousers. I was wearing these corduroy things I mostly just wear to go about. These big bloody holes they have on the knee. So that as well. Christ, I began to think my voice would start erupting in one of these bloodcurdling screams of horror. But no. Did it hell, I was in good control of myself. I glanced down at my shoes and lifted my right foot, kidding on I was examining the shoelaces and that, to see if they were tied correctly. One of those stupid kind of things you do. It's as if you've got to show everybody that nothing's taking place out the ordinary. This is the kind of thing you're used to happening. It's a bit stupid. But the point to remember as well; I was being watched. It's the thing you might forget. So I just I think sniffed and whistled a wee bit, to kid on I was assuming I was totally alone. And I could almost hear them drawing the curtains aside to stare out. Okay but I thought: here I am alone and it's exactly what I wanted; it was what I'd been demanding if the truth's to be told. I'll tell you something as well: I'm not usually a brave person but at that very moment I thought Christ here you are now and what's happening but you're keeping on going, you're keeping on going, just as if you couldnt give a damn about who was watching. I'm not kidding you I felt as great as ever I've felt in my whole life, and that's a fact. So much so I was beginning to think is this you that's doing it. But it bloody was me, it was. And then I was walking and I mean walking, just walking, with nobody there to say yay or nay. What a feeling thon was. I stopped a minute to look about. An error. Of course, an error. I bloody knew it as soon as I'd done it. And out they came.

Where you off to?

Eh – nowhere in particular.

Can we come with you?

You?

Well we feel like a breath of fresh air.

I looked straight at them when they said that. It was that kind of daft thing people can say which gives you nearly nothing to reply. So I just, what I did for a minute, I just stared down at my shoes and then I said, I dont know how long I'll be away for.

They nodded. And it was a bit of time before they spoke back. You'd prefer we didnt come with you. You want to go yourself.

Go myself?

Yes, you prefer to go yourself. You dont want us to come with you.

No, it's not that, it's just, it's not that, it's not that at all, it's something else.

They were watching me and not saying anything.

It's just I dont know how long I'll be away. I might be away a couple of hours there again I might be away till well past midnight.

Midnight?

Yes, midnight, it's not that late surely, midnight, it's not that late.

We're not saying it is.

Yes you are.

No we're not.

But you are, that's what you're saying.

We arent. We arent saying that at all. We're not caring at all what you do. Go by yourself if you like. If you had just bloody told us to begin with instead of this big smokescreen you've always got to draw this great big smokescreen.

I have not.

Yes you have. That's what you've done.

That's what I'd done. That's what they were saying: they were saying I'd drawn this great big smokescreen all so's I could get outside the door as if the whole bloody carry on was just in aid of that. I never said anything back to them. I just thought it was best waiting and I just kind of kidded on I didnt really know what they were meaning.

John Devine

My name is John Devine and I now discover that for the past while I've been going off my head. I mean that the realization has finally hit me. Before then I sort of thought about it every so often but not in a concrete sense. It was actually getting to the stage where I was joking about it with friends! It's alright I would say on committing some almighty clanger, I'm going off my head.

On umpteen occasions it has happened with my wife. Two nights ago for instance; I'm standing washing the dishes and I drops this big plate that gets used for serving cakes, I drops it onto the floor. It was no careless act. Not really. I had been preoccupied right enough and the thought was to do with the plate and in some way starting to look upon it not as a piece of crockery but as something to be taken care of. This is no metaphor; it hasnt got anything to do with parental responsibility. My wife heard the smash and she came ben to see what was up. Sorry, I said, I'm just going off my head. And I smiled.

Margaret's away somewhere

Of course Margaret wasnt the sort of woman you trusted. She had that way of looking at you as if she was wondering how she was going to con you this time and if she could just take it for granted she would get away with it or else did she have to work out methods of escape afterwards. It put you on your guard. And I mean everybody, even the paperboy or the milkboy, when they came to collect the money at the end of the week, they were wary as well. You couldnt help watching her. Even if you were talking to somebody else, if you were standing somewhere where she was, if you were talking to somebody, in the post office for instance, you were always watching her at the same time, so that your eyes might meet and she could go surprised, a bit taken aback, as if she was having to think to herself 'Did he see me there?' but then she would give a wee self-possessed smile and you would give her one back. It was funny the way she managed it, because the truth is she would have won as far as that particular exchange is concerned. And if ever she had to actually say something it would nearly always be a 'What was that?' and this made you know she hadnt been listening to a word you said, this because she rated you so low there was nothing at all you could say would ever interest her, whereas probably you thought she had been waiting for you to speak to her all the time. It wasnt easy being in her company and you were always glad to see the back of her, I mean relieved. But it didnt dawn on me she had disappeared till a long time after – I mean when you told me about it, about how she hadnt been around for a while, it hadnt dawned on me.

Direct Action

From the anglo saxophonics tae the northern germanics, the africs, the asiatics and antarctics, all whatever, I aye get mixed up. It should all be there in black and white so we can check wurselves out, us poor auld indo-europes, we never know if we are coming or going. Of course we have got nay grounds for complaint. I dont care if it is present either in all these shit history books that get written cause it isnay us writes them, it is them writes them, imperialism and colonisation and all the genocides, letting these ruling aristocratic ranching mafia wasp fuckers do what they like not only to their ayn wee children but to everybody else in the world, that is the nub. I dont blame the ruling elites because that would be to give universality the benefit of the doubt. I blame the underlings, not killing the rich bastards, not wiping them out I mean to say it's inadmissible behaviour, shucking off the blame through a so-called inability to take things into their own hands, because they never gie ye the okay to fucking kill them, themselves I'm talking about, gieing ye the okay to do it, the deed.

That was what happened in other countries, the good folk do in the evil baddy bastards unless they get stopped. All the Yankees. Ye want to fucking giggle man know what I'm talking about, uncontrollable. Working-class americans I'm talking about, yous fucking mob man, still waiting for the rulers to gie you the nod jesus christ incredible. Put us out wur misery! Put us out wur misery! Why dont yez make a decision for a change? an adult one, as of a mature being, a fucking intellect, a proper intellect. Yez've been living in bad faith for a hunner and fifty fucking years. Mair.

Once ye learn that you will have understood how come the rest of us wind up on the steps of the presidential palace, having a piss up agin the wall. That's what I'm talking about.

A Memory

O mirs! And a slice of square sausage please!

Beg pardon?

I squinted at her. A slice of square sausage – she didnt have any idea what I was rabbiting on about. A piece of absentmindedness, I had forgotten I was in fucking England. But too late now and impossible to pretend I only said 'sausage' and that maybe she had misheard the first bit, something to do with 'air' or 'bare' maybe, 'scare', 'fare' – sausages are excellent fare I could have said but structured as excellent fare sausages, although the strange syntax would probably have thrown her.

Square sausage? She was frowning, but not unkindly, not hostilely, not at all, this lass of not quite tender years.

It's a delicacy of Scotland.

You what . . .

It's actually a delicacy, a flat slice of sausagemeat approximately 2 inches by 3, the thickness varying between an eighth of an inch and an inch . . . making the movements with both my hands to display the idea more substantially.

The girl thinking I am mad or else kidding her on in some unfathomable but essentially snobby and elitist way. It's fine, I said, just give me one of your English efforts, these long fat things you stuff full of bread and water – gaolmeat we call them back where I come from!

She was still bewildered but now slightly impatient.

Glasgow sausage manufacturers could earn themselves a fortune down here eh! Ha ha.

Yeh, she said, and walked off to the kitchen to pass in my order.

But at least she had answered when spoken to and not left me high and dry. When you think about it, imagine having to take part in such a ridiculous conversation! And yet this is how so many parties have to earn a living. One time I was aboard a public omnibus and dozing; it was a nice afternoon and the rays from the good old sun streaming in the window there. An elderly chap of some seventy or so summers sat nearby. The bus was fairly empty. The driver, a rather brusque sort of bloke I have to confess, and taking it slowly in an obvious attempt at not gaining time. At one point he stopped altogether and applied the handbrake and he sat there gazing ahead, his elbows resting on the steering wheel. Suddenly the elderly chap turns at me and he has to lean threequartersway across the damn aisle so you thought he was going to fall off his seat! He gesticulates out the window in the direction of a grocer cum newsagent shop. You see that there, he says, that shop there, he says, you see it?

Yep.

Well there used to be a cigarette machine stood there, right outside the door.

Is that right?

Aye. He nodded, giving a loud sniff of the nose, then sat back again without further ado. From the way he had performed the whole thing he was obviously a nonsmoker. But even this deduction is a boring try at producing something not so boring from something that is utterly beyond the defining pale even as a straight piece of abject boredom. If the old fellow had simply leaned over the aisle and whispered: Cigarette machines . . . just starkly and in a low growling voice and left it at that, well, I would still at this very moment in my life be incredibly interested in just what precisely the full set of implications

The lass returns the lass returns!

Tea or coffee?

Tea please; and make it two thanks, one just now and one during. Mirs, the age of sauce the age of sauce!

She did not reply to that last bit though, mainly because I managed to stop myself saying it out loud thank the Lord.

Manufactured in Paris

Whole days you spend walking about the dump looking for one and all you get's sore feet. I'm fucking sick of it. Sweaty bastarn feet. I went about without socks for a spell and the sweat was worse, streams in my shoes. Shoes! no point calling them shoes. Seen better efforts on a – christ knows what. Cant make you a pair of shoes these days. More comfort walking about in a pair of mailbags. A while ago I was passing a piece of waste ground where a few guys were kicking a ball about. On I went. We got a game going. Not a bad game. I kicked the stuffing out my shoes but. The seams split. Everybastarnthing split. Cutting back down the road with the soles flapping and that. And I had no spare pairs either by christ nothing, nothing at all. Then I found a pair of boots next to a pillarbox. This pair of boots had been Manufactured in Paris. Paris by christ. They lasted me for months too. Felt like they were mine from the start. I had been trying to pawn a suit that day. No cunt would take it. We dont take clothes these days is what they all said. Tramped all over the dump. Nothing. Not a bad suit as well. This is a funny thing about London. Glasgow – Glasgow is getting as bad right enough. They still take clothes but the price they give you's pathetic. I once spent forty-eight quid on a suit and when I took it along they offered me three for it. Three quid. Less than four months old by christ. A fine suit too. 14 ounce cloth and cut to my own specifications. The trimmings. That suit had the lot. I always liked suits. Used to spend a fortune on the bastards. Foolish. I gave it all up. It was a heatwave then as well right enough but an honest decision nevertheless.

The Place!

Deep water. I want to float through breakers and over breastroking across uplifted by them. This is what I need. And upon the deep open sea. Freshwater wont do. Where are the breakers in freshwater. None. You dont fucking get them. I want to be by a sheer rockface. The steep descent to reach the sea where at hightide the caves are inaccessible by foot alone. I have to startle birds in their nests from within the caves. At hightide the rockplunge into the deep. That is what I want. That. I can swim fine and I can swim fine at my own pace and I have no illusions about my prowess. I'm not getting fucked about any longer.

There is a place I know on the coast. I cant go there. It is not in reach. The remains of a Druid cemetery close by, accounts for a few tourists. The tourists never visit the Place. Maybe they do. But it isnt a real reason for not going. There are real reasons, real reasons. My christ what a find this place was. I climbed down a dangerous part of the rockface. Right down and disregarding mostly all I know of climbing down the dangerous parts. Only perhaps 25 feet. The tide was in. I wanted to fall in. I wanted to dive in. I did not know if it was safe to dive in. If there were rocks jutting beneath the surface. So I did not want to dive in. I wanted to fall in and find out whether it was safe for diving. But if I fell onto submerged rocks I might have been killed so I

did not want to fall in at all for fuck sake which is why I
clung at shallow clumps of weedgrass, loose slate; and it
was holding fast, supporting me, the weight. I kept getting
glimpses of the caves. Impossible to reach at hightide except
by swimming. When I got down to where I could only go
I saw the rocks in the depth and had to get away at that
moment seeing the rocks there I had to get away at once
and each grain of matter was now loosening on my touch
my toes cramped and I had to cling on this loose stuff
applying no none absolutely no pressure at all but just
balancing there with the toes cramped in this slight crevice.

An Enquiry Concerning
/Human Understanding

During a time prior to this a major portion of my energy was devoted to recollection. These recollections were to be allowed to surface only for my material benefit. Each item dredged was to have been noted as the lesson learned so that never again would I find myself in the situation effected through said item. A nerve wracking affair. And I lacked the discipline. Yet I knew all the items so well there seemed little point in dredging them up just to remember them when I in fact knew them so well already. It was desirable to take it along in calm, stately fashion; rationalizing like the reasonable being. This would have been the thing. This would have been for the experience. And I devoted real time to past acts with a view to an active future. The first major item dredged was an horse by the name of Bronze Arrow which fell at the Last in a novice hurdle race at Wincanton for Maidens at Starting. I had this thing to Eighty Quid at the remunerative odds of eleven–double–one–to–two against. Approaching the Last Bronze Arrow is steadily increasing his lead to Fifteen Lengths . . . Fallen at the Last number two Bronze Arrow. This type of occurrence is most perplexing. One scarcely conceives of the ideal method of tackling such an item. But: regarding Description; the best Description of such an item is Ach, Fuck that for a Game.

Clinging On

It occurred to me I was awake. From here was difficult. I had to remind myself that the 'that' was absent and its significance, its significance, the 'absence' or non-existence, or negation, and to piece together, or distinguish the several parts. In normal, or regular – I speak of the day-to-day – discourse or communication the sentence would have written as two part comprising two clauses: 'It occurred to me that I was awake.' A writer of prose might well have used a "that" and therefore lost the meaning for the second clause 'that I was awake' slips into a past, or simply different, time-zone. Whereas a poet might have written, or expressed the sentence separated by line-spacing, thus:

It occurred to me

I was awake.

Finer prose-writers are wary of making use of the poet's devices. They do so, but cautiously. What is clearer now is the separation between the two clauses is not just ambiguous but offers a minimum two meanings and these may be conjoined principal statements: 'It occurred to me' and 'I was awake'. And might be expressed, or written, "It occurred to me (I was awake)." The difficulty is the use of brackets suggesting a banality which amounts not to tautology but, upon examination, of one statement the other may be found. Nought can occur if one is asleep. If the act of occurrence has occurred then certainly one is awake.

Following this I can express it thus: 'I was awake; this realization had taken hold of me' and, the corollary, that I might be expressed as a sentence; if so the use of the term "might" is the key to the evaporation of the space between us (me and reality). From here it follows that I may or may not be so expressed. I was aware of that. Oh God.

A Friend

She was a friend. I knew by her absence. So much that was her, the imprint she left. Hers appeared a gap in space but was a movement. By virtue of that, courses of action, how these are performed.

I learned about music. She was younger than me when she died, younger than I am now. The way I see it she did die even though technically she did not. She was not killed. Imagine 'killed', a woman killed.

She was breathing beyond the accident so that she might have died. She would have smiled as she did so. She was special.

I was not present. In discussing her absence I was hearing music. This was a development. My own life, it too, it has developed.

Her absence and music there someplace, music, filling the absence.

A thought is not a finished entity if it is not one. A thought. Thoughts are more varied. Thoughts; entities in my head, inside it. So that was it too, thinking of her and her absence.

. . .

Difficulties, what we say of it, speaking of it.

And not able to get to it. I can not get to it, to her. And to her, what of her? I can not get to her, reaching to her, reaching her. It is too painful; memories, image. Neither an image, not a thought. She was a friend. Her smile was to me, hers to me.

That's where I'm at

Then there's that other case. I'm talking about the hopeless one we can all get into at some stage or another. Usually it's with a pal we've had for years, when he's pissed drunk and you're no; and you notice everybody's all staring, they're staring at the two of yous. It's when that happens the bother starts and things get quite interesting. You get the boost. It's exciting, it's the excitement, the heart starting to go and it affecting the whole body; you feel the shoulders going and if you're a smoker you're taking the wee quick puffs on the fag, sometimes no even blowing out the smoke, just taking the next yins rapid, keeping it buried deep down, letting it out in dribs and drabs, a wee tait at a time. It's because you're trying to occupy yourself. You're no wanting to seem too involved otherwise it all starts too quick; you want to calm things down, because you know what like you are. That's how as well that you can try and kid on you're no aware of what's happening. When it's a betting shop you're in you act as if you're totally engrossed in the form for the next race. If it's a pub you stare up at the telly. The broo, well ye just stare maybe at the clock or something. But all the time you're keeping that one eye peeled, watching your pal, if he's making a cunt of himself and getting folk upset. Bastards. You're just waiting, trying no to notice, trying to concentrate on other things. Fucking useless but you know it's going to happen; there's nothing you can do about it. Sometimes the waiting doesni even last that long. You're so wound up ready to go you just burst out and fucking dig up some poor cunt who's probably no even been involved in the fucking first place! And you're at him ranting and raving:

You ya fucking snidey bastard ye what's the fucking game at all?

And he's all fucking taken aback: What d'you mean, he says.

Dont fucking give us it, you says.

But I'm no doing fuck all.

Ya lying bastard ye you're fucking on at my mate there you're fucking out of order.

What? he says.

And you start shouting: If ye fucking used your fucking eyes you'd see he was drunk ya bastard!

What! What d'you mean!! I'm just standing here having a pint minding my own business.

Minding your own business fuck all, you shout at him. And the poor cunt now can hardly speak a word cause he's bloody feart, he doesni know what you're going to do, if you're going to fucking batter him. And he looks about the boozer for support, for somebody that knows him to defend him maybe. But nobody does. They dont actually know what happened. They never saw fuck all and dont really want to get involved. They're no really that interested anyhow, when it comes down to it, especially if it's the betting shop it's happening in because they're just waiting for the going behind call so's they can rush over and make their bets. In fact they're probably just watching what's happening to pass the time. There again but some of them will be interested, they maybe know the bloke you're digging up. They might even be the guy's mucker for all you know! But you're no caring. You dont actually give a fuck. It could even make things better. What also happens with me at a certain point is how I suddenly step out my skin and I can look down at myself standing there. Only for a split second though, then I'm back inside again and so fucking wound up I dont notice a single thing, nothing. I wouldnt even notice myself, if I was standing there and I actually was two people. One time I turned round and gubbed a polis right on the mouth. I didnt even fucking notice he was there. He tapped me on the shoulder and I just turned round and fucking belted him one, right on the fucking kisser man and he dropped, out like a light, so I just gets off my mark immediately, out the door and away like the clappers, and poor auld Fergie – that was my mate – he wound up getting huckled; and what a beating he got off the polis once they got him into the station! Poor bastard. But that's where I'm at, that kind of thing, the way it seems to happen to me. It never used to. Or did it? Maybe it did and I just didni notice because I was young and foolish and a headstrong bastard whereas now I'm auld and grey.

Leadership

But for myself it was the greater challenge. The others might see it as theirs, as strangers to this practice. Not me. Never! They would begin, they would buckle down, draw strength from a trial shared. I admired and envied them for it.

My admiration was not misplaced though it surprised them. Of course they looked to me. I was the exemplar, the wonderful exemplar. For some I was glorious. Yes. And why? Because each manoeuvre lay within my grasp. So they presumed, failing to realize such mastery presents not liberation but a vast obligation; a world of obligation, overriding everything. Not only was my own life in thrall to the quest but the lives of those dearest to me.

Some chose not to see this, not to acknowledge the obligation. I cannot name them. Individuals are not functions. I accept this. At the same time they have roles, and enact them. At the same time they look to their own humanity; it is from here we begin.

I regret if they are hurt by such honesty.

It is true also that I smiled. I would not deny the smile. This too surprised them.

Irony is to be shared. To whom did I share the smile? To whom would the smile be shared. None. I was alone. They said I was alone and were correct, an irony in itself, but unimportant if not insignificant.

Then Later

Naybody was aboot hardly and I was hearing my ayn footsteps on the cobbles. I came out frae the back lane gon quite quickly but at the same time pacing myself. Somebody watching wouldnay know how far I had come, a couple of miles or just roon the corner. Ower my left arm was the coat, I had it folded – which didnay seem right somehow, even the way I cerried it was wrang, I knew it; but what could I dae? Maybe if I had slung it across my shooder it would have looked merr the part, but I wasnay that bothered. I crossed ower the wee path up by the canal bridge. The grass was soaking wet and there was piles of litter scattered ower the grun and further on a couple of lumps of shite beside the fence, human shite, at least that was what it looked like. Some dirty bastard. Then another pile of rubbish stacked in among the ferns – including a stack of rubbers, like a gang of weans had fun a gross and startit blawing them inti balloons.

I waited afore heading up and along the canal bank cause ye never know. And frae there ye can see a good wey away. I kept at a fast walk, needing to get out of sight quickly, there was almost nay cover at all noo, no on this side, anybody looking from the road below would have spottit me a mile away fuck, easy. When I got to the lock I had the coat bundled up and gripped in my left hon. I stooped like I was gony tie my shoelaces but I was wanting to see if the coast was clear. This is a point it can be tricky, ye can be too impatient, or else forgetful, ye think ye're hame and dry. I was doubly careful cause of it, I knew other cunts had fuckt up right at that very moment. I didnay care how long it took, within reason. I had the message oot by the tip of the handle. I let it drap and it went plopping doon inti the rushes just oot frae the bank. I couldnay resist waiting an extra second. Even daeing it I knew how stupit it was but ye know the wey it goes, that funny feeling ye're gony see it bounce back oot again, then go jumping alang behind ye, and ye dont know it's there, no till whenever, whatever – stupit – but yer heid's gon in all directions, the closer ye get the merr nervous ye ur.

So ower the lock, and that good smell; for me anywey it's a good smell, I know it's fucking detergent and aw that; but there's something aboot it. Plus cause it's sae open, ye get a breeze. Nay matter. I cerried on in the direction of the Methodist Church. This route led me oot frae between two gable-ends. I got there and then came a loud rattling noise, a lorry. I stood still. It was a delivery wagon. The driver was sterring at me. I gave him a nod but he didnay nod back. For some reason that annoyed me, it really did, fuck you ya bastard, I sterred back at the cunt. I cannay explain it, fucking idiot bastard. Nay kidding ye but the smoke was coming oot my ears. I dont know what the fuck it was to dae with. Maybe gratitude or something. I know it's stupit and there's nay reason behind it. Gratitude? I know. What can ye dae but, ye're just telling it, getting it oot. It's best getting it oot. Nay point letting it fester. Anywey, soon enough there was nothing I wantit to dae. Nothing I felt I should be daeing. Then I was walking. And I got this great feeling. It was cause I had left the driver cunt. I had met him and had the wee minor altercation, letting him see what I thought and aw that, and then when it came to the crunch I just left him stonning, I just fucking turned, no even smiling, nothing, I just fucking turned, that was that, I left him stonning, I left him to get on with it, his fucking deliveries. See if that hadnay happened, if the cunt hadnay reacted the way he had, I really dont think I would have got hame in the right frame of mind; something would have steyed unfinished. Definitely. It sounds shite but that was the wey it was. I felt strong as fuck. Mentally as well. It was June tae and that's something, the sky was fucking great, total blue. Ye felt like gon hiking or fucking climbing; maybe if ye had a bike, take yer stove and some grub.

I watch for signs all the time. The least out the ordinary thing, ye're aye thinking this is the ane, this is the fucking ane, this is it. And see when it isnay! Hoh, jesus christ.

It doesnay matter aboot the coat. Curiosity killed the cat. So they say anywey.

this is different

talking about the weariness, the feeling of fatigue, having to raise yourself off the chair, up off the chair, fighting to raise yourself, and if you manage it, to get yourself up from the chair and are still feeling bad then okay, just go to bed, go upstairs and lie down; switch on the radio, and next on from there – whatever, whatever you need, it is a need, the recognition

but I could not manage it. My eyelids closed and I sighed: a weary irritation, self-irritated, oneself, untrusting in oneself: was I really too bad to rise from the damn chair? or was I pretending, did I have a few gasps before the last, the penultimate

Does it matter, if beyond it, was I beyond it, I was beyond it.

Music, okay, trying that. I thought I was incapable but ahead lay the barrier and through it I would go, I would to go, I willed such.

Later I thought I heard the outside door, someone there and knocking loudly and this was so beautiful; in the act itself, beauty in the act. I would rise, indeed required to rise, seeing who was there but no, I was incapable, I lay back on the chair. The knocking ended. Whoever, whomso, might it have been, could it have been, whomso

friends, and had family, whoever was there. I wondered and to worry, would to have worried.

the tired tired, of tiredness, acutely so. It was acutely so. I could only lie, on the chair, the back on the chair, armchair, a comfortable armchair, the great comfort of it.

When had I experienced this before? It was an acute weariness, an acute weary ness, I

if someone had known, if it was known, I was here.

When Annie was with me

It was fine for her, she fell asleep. She did this in the middle of a conversation. I was flummoxed. Then too the word 'body' as she used the word: or the word cropping up as between she and I, she and he, the 's' nuzzling the 'he', 'body', I was thinking 'bawdy' and writing 'bawdy'. It was that period in our relationship when all she had to do, only the one thing, whatever that might be, thus that the gist, lost forever, so I cuddled her immediately, I always did, and hardons, Annie.

People can disbelieve me if they wish. It was the same where we lived in that old part of the city. I drank in a restaurant whose management hated the sight of us. When asked the nature of my employment, as they put it, how I earned my living, and I told them they smiled sarcastically. When I added, It's true! I would see Annie wince. And so I stopped doing it.

By then she had moved in with me. We were heading to the west coast, we hitched a lift on the outskirts of a village named in the old language, and translated by the locals as 'Cadaver' which I thought interesting and wanted to use. At the same time we were glad to pass through swiftly. I said we should return, the place had a feel to it that I thought creative and I thought lyrics might have been easier to work from within.

Except then, when winter came so too the horrors of such wind, oh the wind, in this part of this country, downpours, the downpouring, freezing rain. Annie was just like Oh God surely it will stop, and was she referring to me rather than any natural element. That made me smile, and became a verse.

But it was not true. I knew I was hearing things, her body on mine, until that moment, not until that moment. We were in a licensed so-called restaurant for a few drinks, it being well in among the wee hours, after hours. It cost someone a fortune. Was this laid on by the organizers? Who knows. She was not acquainted with them, none of them, the folk surrounding, none. And I knew nothing; I never knew nothing, I was just nothing. I was nothing!

So I was in favour, if she was in favour.

It would be boring as hell but we had thirsts to quench, hunger to appease, time to kill. It was me they were watching, and they kept on with it. I did not grudge them the watching. How could I? It would pass. It did pass. Just let them keep out my road, I whispered.

Annie winked, nearly. She said that she had not winked, if so it was unintentional; a wink more a blink. I found this hard to believe but accepted it, that I should not lay such heavy significance on a minor example of 'life instances' which was her name for this phenomenon. She called it an example of a life instance.

I was always smiling when I was with her. There was that thing always, she just made me smile, no matter how tough the moment, being trapped in here and out in there. The rescue arrived. How come! Somehow it did, it always did. That was Annie; that was the great thing.

The Witness

As expected the windows were draped over with offwhite curtains, the body dressed in the navyblue three-piece suit, with the grey tweed bunnet on the head. Drawing a chair close in I sat smoking. I noticed the eyelids parting. The eyes were grey and white with red veins. The cigarette fell from my fingers. I reached quickly to get it up off the carpet. A movement on the bed. Scuffling noises. The head had turned. The eyes peering toward me. There was not a thing I could say. He was attempting to sit up now. He sat up. I placed a hand of mine on his right forearm. I was trying to restrain him. He wanted to rise. I withdrew my hand and he swivelled until his feet contacted space. I moved back. His feet lowered to the carpet then the rest of his body was up from the bed. He stood erect, the shoulders pushed back. The shoes on his feet; the laces were knotted far too tightly. I picked the grey tweed bunnet up from where it now was lying by the pillow and passed it to him, indicating his head. He took it and pulled it on, smoothed down the old hair at the sides of his head. I was wanting to know if he was going to the kitchen: he nodded. Although he walked normally to the door he fumbled on the handle. He was irritated by this clumsiness. He made way for me. I could open the door easily. He had to brush past me. The cuff of his right sleeve touched my hand. I watched him. When he got to the kitchen door he did not hesitate and he did not fumble with its handle. The door swung behind him. I heard his voice cry out. He was making for her. I gazed through the narrow gap in the doorway. He was struggling with her. He began to strike her about the shoulders, beating her down onto her knees; and she cried, cried softly. This was it. This was the thing. I held my head in both hands.

Human Resources Tract 2:
Our Hope in Playing the Rules

The Crime has Occurred.

A crime is a criminal act. We should not have committed the act. If we had not committed the act the crime would not have occurred. We did it. Thus we committed the crime. We cannot 'take it back' as some will suggest. Colleagues think it possible, it is not possible. Actions cannot be undone. We can regret the performance of such an action if it is we who performed such. The deed, however, is done and none travels back in time. We might wish to withdraw the action but that is impossible. Actions may not be withdrawn.

Of our guilt none may know. Not in this world. This is a remarkable feature. We should pause and take proper cognisance of it. Some will ponder the causal relationship. Might we have effected the end result? At all costs it will be known that no consequence shall be suffered. The action we have performed will be known by others. It may or may not be considered a 'crime'. Whether or not the action accords to the term 'crime' is a judgment in itself and outwith our scope. Should this prove the case it will be recognized as our decision, acknowledged as our decision, respected as our decision.

Others will not judge for us. This will not happen unless so allowed. Whether or not people agree with us is of a certain significance but without bearing, unless so allowed.

We may believe ourselves guilty of having committed an action that we should not have committed. We know that in the judgment of other people our action was no crime. But this is not enough for us. We know that we committed a wrongful action and further may believe ourselves guilty of a crime (see para 1). Our quest begins from there and will reveal inconsistencies. Nothing is more certain. In petty detail truths are revealed. Our more risible judgments will have derived from sentimental generalizations.

If we remain in guilt we cannot be with God and may not enter His province. The process of absolution begins with our acknowledgement of guilt. We confess our guilt. It is only through this confession of guilt that our guilt becomes known. In order that we may be absolved our guilt must be known. We confess our guilt to God. This is achieved through direct communication by prayer and other spiritual methods. The magnitude of God's greatness is forever beyond our ken and cannot be a concern.

In many religions there are human mediators who assist us in our quest for absolution. If we are uncertain how to go about matters then the mediators will advise and guide us. A list of those is readily available. They are thought more knowledgeable than ourselves. They are to have received training in the ways and means that direct communication with God may be obtained. The ultimate end is the ultimate mystery. Mediators are taught this most difficult of roles; that which appears to approximate to 'an acquisition of the will to win the attention of God'.

Confessing the crime in theological terms is an important solution and we should not hesitate to embrace such. Our preference is towards these religions into which most of us are born, that place humankind close to the heart of the universe. The heart of the universe is God and His is a beating heart. The centre of the universe is the province of God. God is primary and ultimate dispenser of justice. This alone is our foundation.

Yes we committed the crime. Our examiners may be notified.

Out There

I had to do something new. My way of operating was not so old yet I seemed to have forgotten how to do anything else. I didnay like that. My eyes kept closing too. I was not requiring to sleep, not thinking about sleep at all. Although it was in sleep the thoughts came. I didnay want these thoughts but I got them. And I could not care less if I was caught in the act. I had given up worrying about this months ago, several months ago, last year at least.

Mental preoccupations, I couldnay afford them either. Waves of sleep but I would not allow them to engulf me. Waves of sleep.

I looked for my diary.

It was around somewhere, roundabout – where?

Reflections.

My diary, reflections. Also the usual aches; how come these aches all round my right ear itching and fiddling footering scratching and oh jesus the back side of the head; right side, and just aching, oh fuck. Finding myself in the same old situation was less than helpful. I needed something new and to hell with it.

But in a new form? No, I didnay think so. I didnt

think at all, I didnt, just that, no, not such that I couldnay handle it, and readily, reserving my energy for the struggle itself, not the conditions toward it, setting them for what lay ahead, that was the danger, constant temptation similar to giving up, the concession to it oh god I could no longer just be here, and

just being here.

Although I would be walking into the new place soon. I would be arriving there. So I would keep on. I would. This is not proper decision-making, only a function, continuing as a person.

I knew more was demanded. So what? I knew myself inside out. To be upright, the one deep breath, opening the eyelids to greeting the day. Extant, that was what I looked for, having become, become it: extanticity.

But the temptation oh god and to make it as a question: Why do my eyes close? No, I do not believe it; I do not accept it. All the time they were closing. So what? That is nothing, that is bloody nothing.

I wasnay supposed to sleep. I knew that I could, if I lay down and the scene had been set but how, how, colder, to sleep.

I didnt want even to be doing that, and if it was cold – colder, okay, then my eyes

The Small Bird and the Young Person

– as for example were a Small Bird to thud into your face. Consider the following: a Young Person is chancing to stroll upon an island somewhere in the Firth of Clyde. THUD. A Small Bird crashes onto the bridge of the nose of the Young Person. The day has been fine, a mid-afternoon with an Autumnal sun warm enough to enable the coat to be discarded should the breeze die. Now, the idea of ducking to avoid the collision will never have occurred to the Young Person for quite often you will come to find that birds do fly on courses indicative of just such a collision. At the last possible moment, however, they will dip a wing sufficiently to swerve off. Not this time! While the Young Person is staggering the Small Bird will drop to the ground and lie still, its feathers stiffly spread. Having covered face with hands the Young Person will, in time, withdraw the hands for an examination of the person. But effects to the body will almost certainly be minimal; a little blood, the slight cut, a possible temporary swelling. And nothing else, apart from the stunned Bird. While the view hereabouts will be extensive the Young

Person can see nobody in sight. After a moment the spread feathers begin fluttering; soon the Small Bird starts rising in helicoptereal fashion. Staring at it with furrowed brow the Young Person will turn suddenly and yell, before dashing headlong in the direction of the shingle shoreline.

A Drive to the Highlands

Space was necessary. Not as always but there and then. I come from a large family and space is the one unmistakable entity, people might say, necessary entity. Yes but not for this. I could think of the Highlands and those empty places, empty mountains and hills and the entire area roundabout the lochside. I was not used to it and would have given my eye-teeth to become used to it. But at that precise moment I needed gone from here and there, there was the place. Nothing to do with anything except that. But was it possible?

All morning I thought about it. By the time I was having the pre-work shower I still was thinking about it, I could not escape the fantasy, and since now a thought it was do-able, ergo.

I had a pal, Carl. He had a car. I texted him. Fancy a drive?

Yeah man fifteen.

Quarter of an hour. That was the brilliant thing with Carl, he didnt bother about stuff hardly at all. If ye asked him to do something it was aye or naw, aye if he could, naw if he couldnay. I walked round to his place. I saw he was inside the car already. Fancy a drive up the Highlands?

Okay.

How come you didnt come round and get me? I said.

He nodded his head. He understood the question but didnt have an answer.

Anyway, I said, I liked the walk. I wasnay sure if ye were working today. Good you werent.

I was working, supposed to be.

Me too. Hell with it, just to think and breathe air, real air, breathing real air, air from the deep lochs and wind, wind. In the city you dont get it, not a real wind erupting from the depths of these inland lochs where the water gushes from the depth of the earth rather than the oceans and the ice-floes breaking around the Arctic. Are ye listening?

Carl nodded slightly, staring out the window. By now we were on the road. He hardly spoke at all, especially driving. If he was thinking at all, in opposition to me or not. He never showed it. No matter. Just that face; the concentration. But was it? Maybe it wasnay. Maybe he wasnay thinking anything at all, never mind original, an original thought. Ye never knew with Carl. With me but I was full of thoughts and ideas and all sorts that never came to nothing, Nothing. Never. Who cares. I didnay and neither did Carl. He just joined in. Whatever plans. Anything and everything. All kinds. Not so much plans even just like, just like whatever. I was never a guy that plans. Never ever. What is the opposite of plans. I didnt have plans. Except weird sort of thoughts and ideas and kind of weird, immediacy, immediate, immediate moves, moves to make right at this moment in this here and now. Imagine a hitchhiker, I said, and she had a pal. Two girls, from Switzerland or someplace. Imagine that and they wanted a hitch with us, they just like . . .

Carl smiled.

You maybe know why I said Switzerland but I have this notion resembling a why, just these good fun girls who dont need future plans. What job do you work at and where do you stay, college or university: fuck all that. So they want to know about you instead of just relaxing, just relax, enjoy the drive, a glass of wine or something, have a smoke, listen to the music. The girls I know cant listen, never ever man ye put on music and sit back but they dont. One minute just, they dont, and they're talking, aye talking, asking a question or whatever, telling ye something, that's what they do. The thing is too, I said, going with the Arctic, why not the Antarctic? How come? I'm thinking about penguins except you dont get penguins, not in the Highlands.

Carl nodded. Yeah, he said, frowning.

I sat back, seeing out the window.

A family meeting

Blood is alright, I said, shite is the problem. Or should I say 'shit'?

I dont care what you say it's a horrible word, said my sister, my younger sister. My brother was scowling at me. But I had to say it. And more. It does depend on the family, I said. That is the trouble. And the trouble is ours. It really is. In some families the veins get clogged with excrement and this is what I wanted to discuss with you this morning, I said. So no point looking at me like I smell.

My brother tried to smile. I stopped him in the act. He was looking at me and I was not looking at him and he was very aware of this. He thought I was trying to put one over him. We arent worth a candle, he said, is that what you're telling us?

Whoever wants to be told. Yes, I am.

Then to hell with you and your problems.

I nodded.

The rest were watching the contest. None responded. I had another brother, two sisters and one sister-in-law. Plus a mother and a father who were not present. This meeting was to have been about them. I was trying to get a discussion going. I had been for

months. Years in fact. It seems like years anyway,
I said, I would be as well talking to that effing
television screen.

Well, if you would stop your swearing, said my
younger sister.

I chuckled.

The cheek of you.

You always have to act smart, said the youngest
one.

My brother shook his head but it was not to be
trusted. This amused me. Even more when he said,
You have some nerve.

Yes well that's this family. I chuckled again. If one
must repeat oneself then I will. Family is family is
family. That creates a problem in itself. I've been
grappling with it for years. You know what? It's now
beyond me.

Who do you think you are? said my younger sister.

One of the weans had a headset on: thump thump
thump, interrupting the progression not just of my
thought but collectively, everybody in the damn room.
We were all affected: thump thump thump. It was
almost funny. A nephew. A cheeky wee bastard. They
said he was independent but it was mair than that.
And this thump thump thump was mair than that. His
father who was my brother-in-law had made it an

issue from earlier days, how if one of our children should be into his or her own world in such a way that it impinged on the sanity of other folk then it was up to them to check their behaviour and they had that right which was not a privilege, it was a right. That was my thinking too.

Nowadays it was wishful.

That was one thing. It was neither a right nor my place to grab the wee bugger by the throat and strangle him but I would to have. That was the right, just to tell him aff. My sister, her son. Who was I to interfere. Her big brother but so what? That was their thinking.

Yes well it was not mine. Not when it drove one fucking bananas. Others could complain to each other. I had nobody. My wife could not bear my family. She could not stomach them. Off she went to see a pal for the day, leaving me to weather the storm. Thus I was alone amongst them.

Where was she anyway? She was never here when I needed her. And I needed her now. She was always herself. That was the trouble. She was never a member of the family. Not this one. She always was herself. It always amused me about her. I chuckled.

You're so smart, muttered my youngest sister.

Sorry, I said, thinking about how now and again

she allows members of this family to creep closer to her – creep being the operative term, although so what, that was family, we are all family and we all creep about, our family, yours mine and whoevers, even her, if it was hers and not mine, and I was sick of it. That is how come I asked for a meeting, I was sick of it, just so sick of it.

This was a general malaise, unaccountable, and no prescription, no medicine never mind medication, I could have done with a drink and to hell with it. To hell with this, I would have said, would have loved to have said, and got up and left, except it was me called the damn meeting.

A Hard Man

The best thing he did was commit suicide. Before he did he apologized, but no one was sure for what. Some thought the act itself, others past misdemeanours. I was not convinced. When I heard he had done it I thought 'kill the bastard', but to whom was I talking? and so what if he was already dead, just what exactly did I mean?

Did _it_ mean anything? Did it matter if it didnay?

Okay not at all, okay, who gives a fuck, okay.

It wasnay me asking these questions. I had long ago ceased talking to myself. Way way back. Stultifying fucking monologues.

I hardly knew him. Talking personally. I thought I did but I didnay. The truth is I didnay like him and had nay respect for him either, none at all.

So what? What? There wasnay anything. There wasnay anything. So he was a hard man, so what? So if I should care, I dont think so.

ONE SUCH PREPARATION

THE INITIAL REBELLIOUS BEARING IS AN EFFECT OF THE UNIFORM'S IRRITATION OF WHICH AMPLE EVIDENCE IS ALREADY TO HAND. BUT THIS KNOWLEDGE MAY BE OFFSET BY THE POSSIBILITY OF BEING TOUCHED BY GLORY. AT THE STAGE WHERE THE INCLINE BECOMES STEEPER THE ONE IN QUESTION STARED STEADFASTLY TO THE FRONT. HIS BREATHING, HARSH AS BEFITS AN UNDERGOING OF THE EXTREME, NEVER BETRAYED THE LEAST HINT OF INTERIOR MONOLOGUE. THERE WAS NO SIGN OF A WISH TO PAUSE AND NOR WAS THERE ANY TO REDUCE OR TO INCREASE PACE. HIS CONTROL WAS APPROPRIATE. THE AIR OF RESIGNATION GOVERNING HIS MOVEMENT CONTAINED NO GUILT WHICH INDICATED AN AWARENESS OF OUTSIDE INFERENCE. IT WAS AT THIS PRECISE MARK THE SATISFACTION EMERGED IN THE PROCEEDINGS. HIS ARMS AROSE STIFFLY UNTIL THE FINGERTIPS WERE PARALLEL TO THE WAISTBAND. HIS GAZE HAD BEEN DIRECTED BELOW BUT HE CONTINUED STARING TO THE FRONT AS IF EXPECTING OR EXPERIENCING A REACTION. WHAT WAS THE NATURAL SUMMIT MIGHT WELL HAVE BEEN INTERPRETED AS OTHERWISE.

Fr Fitzmichael

Outwith the Palace Grounds the sudden reversals were being met by widely differing though often violent retorts. But the worthy Fr Fitzmichael continued to perform his duties in a no less perfunctory manner: at 3.24 a.m. he was awake and set for his first of the day; the second was followed by the third and the fourth. When that time for the sixth had arrived he was to be seen sheltering beneath the large tree near to the Boundary. November is a dismal month. A month of the Spirit. A dismal month requires Spirit. In order that we may progress into the next, more than usual attention is to be given over to entities whose design is Spiritual. Fr Fitzmichael then stretched his arms, he was reclining with his back against the gnarled trunk of the tree; a trio of ants had appeared on the tips of his toes. With a smile he leaned to cuff at them with a flick of his over-garment. Such things are we brought to. The condition being a Triumvirate of Hymenopterous Insects on the tips of one's toes. Hello. His *call* to a passing Brother was greeted with an astonished raising of the eyebrows. He waved. November. A month of the Spirit. Spirit and Dismality are equidistant. The Brother hurried off in the direction of the Palace. So, it would seem the Game is to be up. Fr Fitzmichael's smile was benign. The attention of the Superiors shall be brought to bear heavily. So it must be. The tree contains ants. One enters the Palace Library to peruse the books of one's pleasure. One enters the Palace Grounds to be confronted by unimaginable entities whence pleasure is to be derived in the month of the Spirit. Take an acorn. Place it in the palm of one's hand. Squeeze.

A woman I can speak about

There is a neighbour and I could not speak about her. If I did speak of her what would people say? I think I would be blamed. At the particular time I did not, and would not.

It is terrible and ruthless male practice to speak badly of any woman, old as well as young. I cannot abide males engaging in this, even to hear about it from others. I wish they would say it when I was not in the company, if they have to say it at all. It is such crap.

But I was there when it happened, the better to describe it as factual, so that is that. Yes I can speak of her now. Let me say that we should not shy away from the terrible truth that not only males addressed her in demeaning terms, females did likewise. Their terms were so much worse, so much more demeaning. I thought they were her friends. Supposedly, they were.

They were disgusting. Friends like that are disgusting. Among them were people she would have trusted. Had I been her, well, it is easy to say one thing rather than another.

She was pretty too. All people are, in their own individual way. They say beauty is skin-deep. Especially those who are not. But she was pretty and males would have wanted her. It was not this disgusted me. I doubt even that I was disgusted. We use words as we do, but not always precisely. It was a natural feeling and even a mother puts up with that, otherwise it is breakdown, or suicide.

The inhumanity of it that when it had gone she left no recollection, there was no recollection; nothing lingered· Women vanish from memory. What about these men? I wondered about them. Had they any morality at all· My own mind presents its own anomalies, unique to itself· At crucial intervals I also have no memory. Please God let me not speak of that· Other people thought I was her friend but I was not· It was not through friendship I spoke on her behalf. Here can be misunderstandings but I do not believe this to have been one· I say that now and forever will say it, please God.

The Appearance of Absence

People have 'vantage points'. This was his. He was entitled to his; as entitled to his as anyone. He was not good at games but had the right to play them. He was not, for instance, as good as them, but what difference does that make. It was not his problem. They had theirs he had his. His game interested him. Theirs did not. It concerned a particular psychosis. He was no snivelling coward and had no wish to become one. Nor was he unique. Of course not. All the same, he was singular. Everybody is. He was one of everybody. That is the way he liked it.

There is a fall to that expression, a lilting note or downward loop, giving the statement the ring of truth. The rise is the wakening period; the fall is the return to non-consciousness. He was not obsessive but if there is a truth then seek it out. He may have been a stickler. Games of that nature relate to masquerade. One thinks of a story by E A Poe. He read it in his teens. Poe is an author for youth. So many authors are to be read in one's youth. In the story by Poe the limits are set to one's own existence and youth requires to learn that limits exist.

He saw his life as a masquerade. Day upon day we perform a series of rituals. The set of these rituals is the individual, in singularity. This series exists for each 24 hour period and every individual lives within his and her own series. It is indefinite and the sum of these is the unique being. Upon this personal level death was preferable to life. This was the realization. It had become so for him, inevitably. Others might have life, he desired not so much death as absence: almost absence, having that appearance. He felt this so strongly while walking, and walking by the sea, and by the roar, that lifting and raising, the fall, and other individuals, he saw them walking so slowly, dragging their heels and lingering stares to the horizon as to the world, the far off voyage, their dogs, dogs on the leash, the dogs also, mournful.

That place where now he dwelled was a dreaming world. There is a strangeity, a wistful factor; perhaps a presence: Ballantrae. Stevenson and Poe. This was Ayrshire, for some a mundanity. Adults enter, linger. A place of uncles and aunties. His parents separated when he was young. His Uncle and Aunt had given him a home. Each school term this was the refuge, this was the end of term, if only he could reach end of term. They did this for his good, offering stability at this most difficult period. That his parents might have surmounted their differences and resumed living together. They did not. He could not forgive them. Could anyone?

He was relieved to stay with his Uncle and Aunt. Both were readers, his Uncle especially. It was a vast pleasure to trawl their bookshelves. When the adults learned of his interest they enjoyed talking to him, to the amusement of both.

He and his Aunt wheeled his Uncle around in his wheelchair. She was in her late fifties; it was laborious. The boy was twelve, soon to be thirteen. Theirs was a love-match. Even he could see this. They had two children of their own: each lived in foreign parts, each had families of their own.

Here too is where he discovered 'love-benches', these seats where the names of the dearly departed are localised, those who walked these paths and rested, required to rest, and generalized how it was down through the generations and so, as entering the later years, around this part of Ayrshire, for each bench had stories, many stories, some dark, mysterious trysts, unknown lives, secret desires. True desires were never yearnings. He had yearnings, a yearning. He would not describe it as such until older, and discovered that oblivion was not the state he sought, but rather the state of being almost. Where is he? He is not here. He is *almost* here. Where is he? Must he be some other place?

It was a game with an end and the end was absence. The game itself did not end. He dropped from it, or became so dropped. His participation at an end. He continued to read stories; a pastime rather than endeavour. The distinction casts light, offers illumination. Success might provide commentary on one's own life, one's entire life. In his teens he thought to stand or fall by the reading of certain individuals whose names he preferred to conceal. Suffice to say they were German, if Russian Germans in thought and practice. His suspicions were aroused. They seemed altogether untroubled. Life came too easily, too easily. And on what grounds, he could not say, nor yet conceive, not of these grounds. What were these grounds? People have need of their own. Needs are human. If they cannot obtain such they cannot continue. People are entitled to that. All of us. We have those as a need, and the need is a right, and he would have that right, this was an entitlement, asserted and taken.

Calm down son

Bastard, what was fucking keeping her, this was just a nightmare.

It was me, what happened to me. At college too, where I met her, that was where I met her, I was the harum-scarum student, fucking eedjit, the one who cheeked the dons, the fucking dons man know what I'm talking about, I cheeked them. She perceived alternatives, alternatives, as far as I was concerned, too many, too many. Honest. Fuck. Even now, even now

jesus christ

Mind you, totally dependable, as women go – lasses, as they go, ye just christ almighty go back the way, ye go back the way, ye just like eh

That is it with me, that is me. What happened.

jesus christ,

I'm

nevertheless

it's jumpy, ye get jumpy. That's lasses, lasses are lasses.

It isnay that but it's mair than that, mair than that, just like what happened, what happened, lasses, lasses are lasses – so what lasses are lasses, so what?

Harum scarum. What is that tae I mean college, jesus christ.

She knew. I didnay. Round towers and grass lawns; all that kind of shite, boaters, what's boaters? A fucking boater jesus christ, fucking time man where was she. It isnay enough, one does not go on that way, one doesn't, ye just fucking don't man ye just fucking oh god ye just

because ye don't know, no with her. I don't, never, I never

I was lost with her, without her, just lost and ye are just standing there and

christ knows. Even at college, I never knew, seeing them all, that class thing, class, phantasmagoria, boaters down the river, white dresses and flouncy petticoats, wee umbrellas, in the shirt sleeves, harum scarum in the skiff punting like fuck; oh here she comes; who is she walking to? To whom. Me. Me, walking to me, jesus christ

jesus christ, ye're just fucking

that's what I'm talking about, just like

On Leave

Daniel noticed the baby looking, twisting about on Michaela's lap. But it was looking past him. He followed the look. An old guy on the seat across the aisle making faces. The baby was looking at him. The old guy was smiling. The baby looked like whatever it was, what it was doing in its own face. It just seemed to be looking, trying to figure out the old man, what he was doing. Daniel didn't know either. He had been thumbing the magazine, the adverts; mainly it was adverts. He raised the bottle of water and swallowed a mouthful, returned it into the net compartment on the back of the seat in front.

The old man looking again, it was Daniel he was looking at. Right at him. Daniel didn't react. He turned a page of the magazine. The old guy stopped looking now.

Sometimes his mother did the same, she just looked, seeing things, not meaning anything, not being critical. He hadnt seen her for a while. Probably she was okay. People did that, they looked; that was what they did. The baby, its head lolled, drooping, staring down, he was awake, just staring. What at – the floor. Its head nodded, maybe going to sleep.

A wee bit later and Michaela was holding it up, she was arranging the clothes, to do with that. She saw Daniel and smiled. Daniel nodded. She was doing it now with one hand, holding up the baby, doing the clothes with the other. She managed it easy.

The baby too, looking over her shoulder, the row behind, just looking at something, whatever it was. Daniel shifted slightly to see back over the seats. It was a woman in the row behind who was making faces and smiling then talking: Oh oh oh oh see you see you oh you're a good boy, oh oh oh. The baby was staring at her. His name was Daniel too. Michaela wanted to call him that. Daniel didnt, not really, he didnay really care.

She was finished what she was doing with the clothes, lowered the baby down on to her lap, so it was facing into the back of seats in the row to the front, and its head lolled.

Its wee head. It was sleeping. Maybe its head would get sore.

Daniel reached in to the net compartment, brought out the magazine, thumbed through it again. The watches were good, they were good deals. But he didnay need one. He yawned and shut the magazine, returned it to the net compartment. There was a change in the sound of the plane engine. Michaela gestured to him. Quarter of an hour to landing. Och well. She smiled. Daniel nodded, raising his eyebrows. She was looking past him. That old guy again; nosy old cunt. He was looking at Daniel and smiling. What about? Was he to smile back? Old folk. How come he was smiling? The baby, it was the baby. He was seeing the baby, looking at the baby and the baby was looking at him. That old face. What age was he? You never know with people. Some are old and look young. He winked, the old guy. Its head twitched and a look on its face, his cheeks, the wee boy, and his eyes too, just staring now, staring at the old guy and like he was going to smile then not, then not, his head nodding, looking down: a twitch in his neck, whatever that was, what that was: his neck? Daniel frowned. He nudged Michaela and she gestured, meaning what, he shrugged. The baby, he said.

Here. She smiled and passed him it.

Daniel moved, raised his hands to take it and she gave him it. He with one hand underneath, the other on the shoulder then the other shoulder, so both shoulders. It squirmed, squirming, the baby was squirming but he just held it, he didnt press. He removed his right hand, put it to the side, to the baby's hip, to the waist, its clothes were tight, just tight or the nappy or maybe, whatever, something, just tight, too tight maybe. That whimpering sound, oh God, that whimpering sound. Daniel's eyes blinked. He hated it, babies doing that, he hated it. This whimpering sound it was like crying, it was worse than crying. Daniel held him up, holding him under the shoulders, the armpits. He was not crying, not whimpering either. Daniel squinted at it, looking back at him, just doing that, just looking. Babies did that too.

Flightstaff to landing, something to landing.

Michaela was holding out her hands, the baby dangling, he passed her it.

Then the landing, and the bumps and the rocking and bump bump bump they were down.

The old guy's eyes opened. They had been closed. Maybe he was praying. People prayed. Long flights and they worried. What about? The crash, the plane crashing. Daniel smiled. He reached into the net compartment, lifted out the phone, he began scrolling, and Michaela smiling to him. Daniel nodded. That was them now, the three of them. And the old guy shifted on his seat, trying to see out the window, he couldnt, not from where he was sitting.